25 SERVINGS OF SOOP

Literary Journeys into Life, Meaning, and Love

∾

VOLUME I

25 Servings of SOOP Volume I © copyright 2020 by
Something or Other Publishing, LLC.

ISBN 13: 978-1-7324511-6-2

Library of Congress Control Number: 2020935111
Printed in the United States of America
First Printing: 2020
18 17 16 15 14   5 4 3 2 1

Edited by Catherine Bordeau
Cover design by Dragan Bilic

SOMETHING OR OTHER PUBLISHING
Info@SOOPLLC.com
For bulk orders e-mail: Orders@SOOPLLC.com

CONTENTS

FOREWORD

Mark Twain, one of America's greatest literary treasures, once said, "I apologize for such a long letter - I didn't have time to write a short one."

It takes great skill to tell a story in a way that captures all of the important details while cutting out the fluff. When we discuss our anthology series with authors, many are taken aback by our maximum allowed word count—2,000 precious words. And yet, we've found this call to ration words, to describe only the most important details, and to make every sentence a value-add has resulted in many masterful stories.

We've described 25 Servings of SOOP as a "literary wine tasting of up-and-coming talent." This wine tasting has the sweet rosé of "Frank and Lily" by Sian Fullerton balanced by more intense flavors such as "The Storm in His Eyes" by Charmaine Kimbini and "The Unpainted Portrait" by M.D. Jerome. Heart-warming stories are juxtaposed with stories of absolute horror.

While all of the stories we've chosen to include are quite enjoyable on the surface, many have special notes on which we hope you'll pick up. Many of our authors did an admirable job of subtly addressing social issues. Many stories feature diverse characters and highlight the challenges faced by people who are, perhaps, a little different from us. We, of course, hope you will be entertained by this book, but it's our deepest wish that you will take away from at least one story the desire to understand, respect, love, and empathize with others better.

With gratitude for your support,
Something or Other Publishing

Section One:

Coming of Age

TEA

LAILA EL REFAIE

My first cup of tea hardly had any tea in it. I went up to my grandmother; she had assumed the role of my mother while my real mother was at work. I went up to her and told her, quite boldly, that I wanted a cup of tea. I called her *Mumy Shushu*, a combination between her nickname and a respectful but affectionate prefix. In all my boldness, my six-year-old mind had envisioned a cup of the red, hot substance from which clouds of steam flew up and faded into the air, dancing, colliding, and at last disappearing into the atmosphere in a bold display of grown up-ness. Instead, I was met with a mug of some unknown liquid that looked nothing like tea. Looking at the pale colour, I was confused but thanked the housekeeper and drank it politely.

"We added some milk to it, because it's not good for you to drink it as it is at your age." *Mumy Shushu* explained her decision without me having to ask. I thanked her, beaming as I was reassured that what I had in front of me was definitely a cup of tea, no matter how it looked. I would later discover the enchanting beauty of the clouds of milk that consume every colour but their own when they are poured into a cup. It was warm and sweet, and with that first sip, it seemed that we had attained a new understanding together, a new shared appreciation. With her short, light brown hair, curled neatly around her face, and her small, tender eyes that offered kindness to anyone they looked at, *Mumy Shushu* was a gentle embrace and a shimmering star encompassed in one person. Whether it was at the serving of her tea or at the words of another, her smile was genuine, and I have grown to be just as terrible at hiding my emotions.

She asked me if I liked the tea, and I nodded my head in excitement before drinking the rest of it. *Shay b Laban* became my drink of choice every morning when I didn't have to go to school. I would sit on our green armchair with a small table in front of me and sip at my mug while I told her all about my goings-on, many of which were rooted in my school experiences. She would listen intently, giving me all the attention a listener could give as she sipped her own milk-less tea. How a woman her age could find any interest in the ramblings of a child, I never knew. Her eyes would shift from me, to her cup, then back to me. It was like the whole world had vanished, and all that was left was us and our tea.

When I turned nine, I heatedly asked for my tea without any milk in it. I remember asserting that I was no longer a child, and in that sense, I had the right to my own cup of *proper* tea. *Mumy Shushu* didn't object. I remember it was summer, and I sat there in my pajamas, eagerly awaiting my tea as she made her phone calls to the supermarket and her relatives. I didn't understand most of what she said, but none of it mattered—because when my tea arrived with hers, she set the phone aside. I was silent, waiting for it to cool and moving the cup to my lips every two minutes to see if I could drink it. Every time its vapour would threaten to singe my lips if I brought it too close, I would set it back down, wait a little bit, and then pick it up again. Until finally, it allowed me to try it. The bitter, pure flavour of the tea intermeshed seamlessly with the sweetness of the sugar and descended upon my tongue like an onslaught. Had all this been obscured by one dash of milk? It felt less like something that simply satisfied my tastes, and more like a delicacy that ought to be enjoyed slowly and carefully, lest a sliver of its flavor disappear in the liquid falling through my lips and down my throat.

I took slow and careful sips as *Mumy Shushu* told me one of her many stories about her life, about God's angels, and about the memories of a time I could only experience through her lens of nostalgia.

"*Shoofi ya habebti*," she began. "I spent a long time in Europe, and everyone would always have their tea at five, sharp. But you know me, I could never give up my morning tea, and my cup of *qahwa* at noon." I knew that *qahwa* was another delicacy my tongue would have to wait to savor. "After that, at five,

I would join the ladies for tea." Entranced, I listened as she told me about the different kinds of tea she had tried during her days in Europe, and how each kind of tea had its own distinct taste and flavor.

"What's *your* favourite, *Mumy Shushu*?" I asked as I touched the mug to see if its contents had cooled to drinking temperature.

"I've always liked a good strong cup of English Breakfast. Most people don't change their favourite type once they've found it." She gave me a knowing look as she took another sip of her tea, as though she were predicting which type would be my favourite. It would later turn out to be Earl Grey. I never knew if she was right.

Soon enough, as I grew older, our housekeeper left and was replaced by another who would leave at four every day. This meant that the task of preparing afternoon tea was passed on to me, and I took it upon myself to make every cup as sacred as the time we spent sharing it. She would sit on her sofa and watch a television series or an interview with a celebrity, while I would set up the kettle and place our teabags into our cups. I knew exactly how many mint leaves were needed to accentuate the flavours of each tea (five, but I would sometimes add six or seven if the leaves were especially small) and how many times to shake the teabag in the cup to ensure that it reached the right richness without getting too bitter (four times, then you push it down with the teaspoon for three seconds). I knew how to stir the sugar so that it dissolved almost instantly, leaving no lumps or bits at the bottom of the cup (the trick's in leaving the stirring part to the very end), and the task of preparing tea became something of a talent of mine. "*Teslam eedek.*" *Mumy Shushu* would always say after the first sip before mumbling that if only I didn't have to go to school, then I could make us tea in the morning as well. I silently agreed with her.

Some days, she would explain our family tree to me—"How are we related to *Tante Wagiha* again?" Others, she would answer my questions about religion—"Why do religious people do things that are obviously *haram*?" Sometimes, she would tell me of her adventures in Europe, and her comic stories about learning to speak different languages only after arriving in their countries. My favourite was when she thought a bottle of apple-based cleaner was a bottle of apple juice, when she was in Italy. She would laugh with me, and look at me with all the kindness in the world. I was prepared to die for her, but making her an excellent cup of tea every day seemed like a good enough alternative.

Then she died. When I was twelve, she had to be hospitalised for a problem in her digestive system that I was too young and too afraid to understand. Suddenly, I was responsible for the house while my mother spent her nights in the hospital room alongside her. I was in charge of making sure the food was prepared correctly, of packing clothes for my mother, of making sure that the house was cleaned properly. Even the cats were in my care now. I remember stepping out of my room door one day, and everything was dark. I hadn't had a good cup of tea in weeks. It was mid-afternoon, but there was no sunlight. Winter was drawing near, and the October winds were beginning to howl.

Until the very end, I was sure that all of it would pass. I refused to so much as consider the notion that she could die. How could she? I had to make her tea before I would leave to prepare for my high school graduation, and she would join me later in the evening. She would voice her wish that I didn't have to go to university, then to work, so I could make her tea every day. We would sip our tea over our discussions of my life as it grew more complex with adulthood. And then, when all that was over, I would welcome her into my own home and make her the best cup of tea, as her great grandchildren sat at her feet and listened to her story. All of these things had to happen with her, so there was no way she could die.

But God had other plans, and indeed, He took her from me. He shattered my plans of drinking my next cup of tea with her. She died on the morning of the 25th of November. That morning, I could no longer imagine myself brewing a single cup of tea again, but I did. I made it for my mother, and soon enough, I made one for myself. I placed the Earl Grey tea bag into my cup, and the English Breakfast into my mother's. Then, two lumps of sugar into each cup. Then five mint leaves—they were big leaves—and I poured the boiling water. I shook the teabags, then pressed them to the bottom of the cup for three seconds. Finally, I stirred the sugar until it dissolved, and sat down with my mother for our afternoon tea. It's what *Mumy Shushu* would have wanted me to do.

And yet, as I sip my tea in the morning, my eyes sometimes shift to her place on the sofa, and I wonder what she would say to me over the day's cup of tea. Then, I set down my empty cup, and I go about the rest of my day.

∽

Laila El Refaie is an author and editor with interests in history, phenomenology, ethics, and art. Her writing is mainly focused on fictional short stories, creative nonfiction, and analytical think-pieces. She is now brainstorming ideas for her debut novel, while also trying to learn Latin without summoning a demon—both of which are equally difficult.

DINNER AT GRANDMA'S
ERIC S. MONDSCHEIN

A t least once a month on a Sunday as we were growing up, mom and dad would pack us all into the car, and we would drive from our home in Rockland County, New York, to our grandmother's home in Brooklyn. Grandma was my dad's mom. We did not know my grandmother from my mom's side, as she had passed away when I was one, and we never did meet our grandfathers as they had both passed before my brother, Jeff, and I were born.

We would head toward New York City by first driving through the winding tree-covered roads of northern New Jersey to Route 17, a busy road with stores all along the divided freeway, and it would take us over the George Washington Bridge and down the Westside Highway. When I was eight, we no longer went down Route 17, but instead we took the newly built Palisades Parkway. It was great because it did not allow trucks, and the road all the way to the George Washington Bridge was through the woods and up and down rolling hills. I remember the drive so well because as we neared the bottom of Manhattan, on the West Side Highway, there were many ships docked along the way. Big ships from far away places with foreign flags. The ships were black and white with huge smoke stacks, and they were all painted red where the ship touched the water. My brother and I used to read the names off their bows, names such as the *SS Queen Elizabeth*, the *SS Queen Mary*, the *SS Rotterdam*, and later the *SS France*. Most of all, my brother and I loved seeing the ships from the US Navy that would dock there every so often.

Once we passed the docked ships, I do not remember much else except going through a long tunnel where my mom would always tell us that we were almost there and that my brother and I had better behave or we would be in some serious trouble. As we got close to grandma's, you could only see apartment buildings and homes made mostly of dirty red brick that were attached next to each other from one end of the street to the other. What stood out was that there were almost no trees. Growing up in the country where we did, I could not understand why anyone would have cut down all the trees.

Once we got to grandma's, we walked up three flights of stairs. I could never fathom, and still don't, why people say three flights when you actually go up a set of stairs and then make a turn and then go up another, but that is only counted as one flight. Anyway, once we got to the door, she was always waiting with the door open and ready with hugs and kisses for everyone. I must confess, I did not look forward to that. She would hug me so tight, and I would disappear between her huge bosoms, wondering sometimes if I would ever get out. Then, she would hold my cheeks and pinch them, and yes, it hurt. Each time, she would say, "You are growing up so fast." My brother and I would then walk into the kitchen, and it always looked like a storm had hit it. There were dirty pots and pans stacked up in the sink and all over the counters, and those on the stove were bubbling and steaming. Most of all, I remember the smells; the air was filled with aromas that were warm and rich and so full of promise. Just standing there, I would feel my mouth begin to water as I recognized the different smells of roast chicken, chicken soup, brisket, potato kugel, and her incredible apple streusel.

She would tell us all to hurry, to wash up, and go sit down as dinner was ready. Of course, no matter when we got there, it seemed like dad was always late, even when we would arrive thirty minutes before he said we would be there. Entering her dining room was special. Her table was always covered by a white linen tablecloth and was set with china and crystal and real silverware. I remember how it all looked so very old. My mom would try to tell her she did not have to go to so much trouble or be so fancy, but grandma would always smile and tell her it was no trouble at all. Honestly, I think mom was more concerned about my brother and me breaking something.

The appetizer was already at each place setting: a fish dish, and it was always the same dish—gefilte fish and horseradish with beets. All I will say is that it is an acquired taste. Frankly, with my grandma, it was actually a *required* acquired taste. After everyone finished their fish, and I do mean finished it, grandma would insist that no one get up. She would clear the table and bring the next course—chicken soup. It was one of my favorites. It was real chicken broth, real chicken, sliced carrots, a little celery, and dill and sometimes dumplings. Simple, but there was something she did to that soup that no one has been able to replicate to this day. Unlike our dinner table, not much talking took place, and my brother and I said nothing. We would look at each other and sometimes giggle, but we said nothing. After the soup was finished and the bowls cleared, grandma would bring in the main course. Of course, again help would be offered, but always refused. There was roast chicken, brisket of beef, and potato kugel. She always served a vegetable, and it was usually green beans. The food was delicious, and my brother and I would always get seconds. Dessert was her homemade apple streusel, and she always gave us seconds.

This is how dinners at grandma's would go and what was served each month year in and year out until I turned thirteen. We arrived as usual and were ushered into the dining room the same way every month. One meal, we ate our appetizer and soup as we had done each visit, and she served the main course as she had always done. Then, grandma served me a piece of chicken, some potato kugel, green beans, and added some beef brisket as she handed me my plate. After everyone was served, I cut a piece of chicken, and no sooner had the chicken passed my lips, when grandma put her fork down and looked at me with this hurt expression and said, "So what's wrong with the brisket?" I have to admit that I was at a loss. I did not know what to say or do. I told her I loved her brisket, and at that, she stood up and said she had to get something from the kitchen. As she walked away, she said, "How would you know? You never even tried it." I looked at my dad, seeking guidance on what I should do, and he just continued eating, not even looking up. I felt terrible, but she returned, and we carried on like it never happened.

I may have only been thirteen, but I was no fool. I was a fast learner. So the next month when we visited grandma and were sitting at the table - after the last person had been served the main course, I cut a piece of brisket instead of the chicken. But again, no sooner had it passed my lips, and she asked, "So, what's wrong with the chicken?" With that, she got up, telling us that she had to get something from the kitchen. I again looked to my dad for some kind of direction, and he again said nothing and continued eating. I then looked to my mom, who, like dad, was just eating and not looking in my direction. This went on for several months, and frankly, I was beginning to think that something was just not right with grandma.

The next month we visited grandma, I decided I was going to watch what others did, as they never seemed to upset her. This time after everyone had been served, I began eating, not the chicken or the brisket, but the potato kugel. I surreptitiously watched my dad, and I discovered the secret and the solution to my problem. Dad would cut a piece of chicken and then cut a piece of brisket. Making sure he had a small piece of each on his fork, he would take a bite. After that, he would just eat as he always did. So, that is exactly what I did, and grandma said nothing to me and continued telling my mom and dad about how her week had been.

I looked at my mom sitting across the table from me, and as she caught my eye, she smiled, winked at me, and then proceeded to join the conversation with my dad and grandma again.

∽

Dr. Eric S. Mondschein has taught law and education and published and edited numerous articles and books in the field. He also served as the citizen represent-ative of **The Post Star** *editorial board in 2009 and 2018. He is the author of* **Life at 12 College Road**, *published by Something or Other Publishing, which is a collection of short stories about growing up in America in the 1950s and 60s. He is also the co-author with Ellery M. 'Rick' Miller Jr. of* **Sexual Harassment and Bullying; Similar, But Not The Same**, *and an accompanying Teaching Supplement published by the Education Law Association in 2015. He currently resides in the Adirondack Mountains of upstate New York with his wife, Ginny. They have two grown children, Adam and Emily, a son in law, Kamal, a daughter in law, Yaani, and grandchildren, Annie, Nathanael, and Eli.*

AFTER ALL

KIMBRIAH L. ALFRENAR

As a young kid, I never had the desire to become a writer. When I was four, I wanted to be a doctor (naturally, my parents were ecstatic). When I was five, I decided I was going to be the next American Idol (my parents were less ecstatic, but still supportive). I don't remember exactly what other jobs crossed my mind from the ages of six through ten, but I can imagine it was quite a list.

The one occupation that I am sure had never crossed my mind was "writer." I had never put much thought into who wrote the books I was reading. I had never thought it was possible for *me* to become a writer, let alone a full-blown published author. All I knew was that I loved to read, constantly dragging my dad to the library every other week, and I loved to write, relishing all the creative writing assignments given to me at school.

I always kept a flashlight on the nightstand by my bed, and as soon as my mom said "goodnight" and left my room, I would take it, turn it on, and start reading. This plan worked for quite a while, until one day, my mom decided to come right back in. I can't remember if she forgot her glasses or if she suddenly decided she wanted to do laundry (you'd be surprised how often that happened), but she walked right back in. My young, naive mind thought that if I hid the flashlight under my blanket, she wouldn't notice. That might've worked if I had actually turned the flashlight off. Needless to say, my mom *did* notice the random bright light glowing from beneath my blanket and made me go to sleep.

This love of reading exposed me to many different styles of writing, and like a sponge, I unconsciously soaked up all of the techniques of those writers. In

4th grade, the first year I had to take a standard state-based writing assessment, I was given a lot more writing assignments as practice. Teachers and fellow students began complimenting me, longing for a continuation of stories that I purposefully ended with cliffhangers. I humbly accepted their compliments but never attributed them to a possible sign of the career path I could be taking. After all, I was only nine years old. All I really cared about was Minecraft, the presents I would get on Christmas, and the possibility that the world would end in 2012 (spoiler alert: it didn't).

It wasn't until 5th grade that I got the idea to write a book. Thursday, April 24, 2014, was Take Your Child to Work Day. My parents only worked night shifts at their hospitals, so I never had anywhere to go during the day. They always gave me the option of staying home, but I always decided to go to school.

At my elementary school every year, all of the teachers always had a competition in which the teacher with the smallest amount of kids in his or her class won. They didn't win a prize or a trophy. They just got the satisfaction of claiming their victory. That year, my class lost with six kids compared to another teacher's one (that must've been a quiet school day).

In the middle of the day, my teacher decided to let us go on the computers. At the time, we only had 4 desktop computers available, each about as big as a medium-sized cardboard box. Sadly, I, along with another student, didn't get a computer, but I did get the pleasure of watching my friends mess around and draw ducks out of pixels in a Word document.

One of my friends had the bright idea to "write a book." The book was going to be about ducks (I don't know why, but my friend had a weird fascination with ducks). He never actually started writing though. Instead, he spent the entire time designing a book cover, and, yes, by that, I mean drawing a duck with a top hat out of pixels. But that act got me thinking. All of my teachers and friends thought I was a good writer. Why not write a book?

As soon as I got home, I took my dad's laptop, opened up my own Word document, and started writing "Grandma Dotty." I don't know where the idea came from, and to be honest, I wish I had chosen a more original name than "Grandma Dotty," but that was where I started. I dreamed up a story about a girl named Lily, who was planning on having an amazing summer with her friends (Abby and Daisy, two more generic names). All of her plans were seemingly ruined by none other than Grandma Dotty, her least liked grandparent who always seemed to be allergic to fun and who would sadly be staying with her for the *entire* summer. The two characters had a rough summer start-up, constantly clashing with each other while Mom (never named her) was in the middle trying to make amends. By the end, they bonded over something you probably wouldn't expect and the rest of the summer passed like a breeze.

The story played out in my mind like a movie. Whenever my dad's laptop was free and I was in a writing mood, I would sit down and add to it. I didn't tell anyone that I was writing a book, because I didn't think there was anything special about it. I didn't even know that I could get it published. After all, I was only ten years old. All I really cared about was Minecraft, the presents I would get on my birthday, and the possibility that I could become the next big YouTuber (spoiler alert: I didn't).

When I finally told my mom I was writing a book, she gave me a lecture on plagiarism. After assuring her I didn't copy the story from one of the books on my bookshelf, she started reading it and told me it was good. Assuming she was simply being a supportive mother, I told her, "Thanks!"

She looked at me and said, "No, this is really good! You could get this published!"

Published? No way.

Sure enough, in January 2016, I published my first book. I got overwhelmingly (and to be honest, surprisingly) positive feedback. Everybody thought that my book was "amazing."

I remember my friend telling me, "You wrote this?! It looks like a real writer wrote this! This is like an actual book!"

I replied, "Yeah, that's kinda the point!"

Just like that, in the span of one Take Your Child to Work Day, my career choice changed permanently. I thank God I was at school that day. God is the reason why I do what I do and why I am who I am. I wouldn't be here today without Him. I wouldn't have ever known being a writer was even possible, let alone a full-blown published author.

After all, I'm only sixteen years old. All I really care about is family, getting into a good college, and the possibility that I could become a #1 bestselling author (spoiler alert: I will).

∽

Kimbriah Alfrenar is a 16-year-old Christian, Haitian-American, published author of two books, with **Grandma Dotty 2: SCHOOL!** *coming out soon. She lives in Florida with her younger brother and her parents. Other than writing, she has been playing piano since she was five and also enjoys drawing. She has won awards from the Miami Youth Fair and the Florida Art Education Association for her art pieces. You can find her on Instagram:* @kimisaboss123 *or head over to her website:* briahbooks.com.

THE STORM IN HIS EYES
CHARMAINE KIMBINI

Alexander Jason Demetriou was nothing if not an aberration. As the only child of Aetòs and Clarissa, everyone expected him to present his magic at the normal age of fifteen and not sooner. But alas, Xander's magic presented at the young age of eleven and not in the way everyone expected. His magic didn't course through his veins like other royal children. No, his was a spark—a sharp, precise, yet utterly devastating spark. It resided in the corner of his eyes, giving him complete control over any mark he laid his eyes upon. His was an actual blessing or curse situation.

No one within the royal walls had ever heard of a spark that lit up eyes before. So this resulted in Xander being alienated. So began his journey as the boy who would become one of the most formidable warriors in the kingdom. Unlike most princes and princesses, Xander was not afraid to get dirty, to venture where others dread, and to plunge in with both feet. He always had a certain pull toward darkness, which frightened many of his peers and further alienated him from royal society.

Not only that but when Xander's magic presented, it had been in an unexpected, dangerous way. He had been only an adolescent then, so tantrums were common. But Xander hadn't thrown tantrums before adolescence. He had always been one of those children who sat down in a dark corner and brooded like a sour wolf. Xander brooded like an actual brooding adult: all dark and frightening without a trace of childlike innocence. This time it had been different. Everyone felt the gnawing shudders as soon as his nanny had said, "No." It was as if they could feel the storm roll in, as if something utterly devastating was coming, but they didn't know what. Xander stood in place staring at his nanny as if trying to will her to change her mind. But she had been through his teenage tantrums before, and she held her position and said a louder sterner no.

The tremors were now unmistakable. His eyes changed color, and his pupils had a single unmistakable golden-lightning imprint, as if he were about to rain on the whole household. His hair shimmered with an unmistakable silver edge, and everything slowed down to an excruciating yet frightening pace. He didn't say anything except a silent, "What?" as he glared at his nanny. She felt everything in waves then. The shivers that felt like a thousand spiders crawling up her bare calves, then her arms, and a sliver of ice sliding down her back. It all felt unreal, like a bad plot of a horror movie. Yet as ironic as it was, it ratcheted up her heart rate to a sickening speed. Meanwhile, Xander stood there all-powerfully mad, unyielding, and unmoving as if he were on a boring, mandatory missionary trip.

"Xander," his nanny croaked breathlessly.

But Xander was unyielding in his hold. He wanted what he wanted, and this measly human was not going to stop him. He exhaled a bored breath, and the lightning in his eyes burst into thunderstorms. This turned the blood in her veins into molten magma, hot and uncontrollable. It boiled her skin from the inside out, and every exhale was like a burst of hot air spurting from her mouth. At that moment, she knew the only thing keeping her upright was Xander's unforgiving gaze, and even as she died from the inside, she knew he didn't realize the sheer depth of what was going on yet.

"Alexander!" His father's voice boomed from the corner of the large room instantly stopping the proceedings in the room.

His nanny crumbled to the floor, skin flushed and large welts on her arms and legs. Her eyelids were closed, but the squires who ran in were watching her eyes dart to and fro under her closed eyelids. Finally, it hit Xander. He realized what he had done. He immediately broke into a mess of sobs and said, "I don't know what happened," over and over again as the guilt and confusion enveloped him.

His father had felt his magic draw to his son, and he knew what that meant. It meant Xander had presented, but it did not feel like it should have—not that he would know. His father didn't have another child, but he knew. It just wasn't supposed to feel like that. Xander's magic pull was strong and dark; his father felt Xander's anger pull at his magic like a stubborn dog. Until he had frightened the boy back to his senses. If not tamed, he would use his magic for evil. The solemn king hugged his son and vowed to make it right for him.

After that news made its way through the royal walls, all the workers knew of the boy king who could be dangerous. They told stories of him to the kids they took care of, and this further singled Xander out. At school, no one dared breathe within a five-foot radius of him. The king and queen did not take this well. Whatever they did to help their son did not work, until one day after Serena, the princess of the North Quadrant, presented.

She was merely fourteen years old when she felt the sadness and isolation within Xander. It had almost suffocated her like a blanket of despair and broken dreams. Back then, she did not know what was going on, but she knew this boy was suffering and only she could fix it. She made an effort every day to be around him. Xander was sixteen then, and he was growing up to be an attractive yet intimidating man. Being him was not easy. Girls used to giggle when they glanced at him, whether it was because of his 'assassin king' story or his now handsome face, he never knew. But with Serena it was different. She smiled at him like she knew him—all of him. Like there was no need for walls or pretense. After five years of pushing everyone away, Serena was the first who refused to be pushed away. She always came back. Soon enough, the light in her had filled the blank spots that the darkness had not reached in him.

She brought out a feeling of balance in him. His whole aura felt full around her. When he went out for his war training activities, she always tagged along. She always managed to stay within arm's length. When he had healing classes (because with magic like his, he was bound to hurt someone accidentally), she sat beside him and kept him company. It was only during advisory classes that she left, because she had ruling classes. Even though ruling classes were for all first-generation royals, Xander's father thought the power would distort his judgement, so Xander took the advisory class instead. The classes were the same except for maybe a few key things, like when to ignore your subjects and when to use your ethics against your wishes.

By the time Serena turned fifteen, she discovered that Xander had been her soulmate and that pull she felt was nothing if not consistent. The stories her parents told her about being soulmated all made sense now: the pull, the hunger, and the intense emotions. Wherever she went, whatever she saw, everything brought forth memories of him, and the tug in her heart towards him grew. Xander was the most avoided guy in school, and she was the most popular girl in the school. They balanced each other out. This was most necessary, since their magic was completely opposite. Dark and light. Fire and ice. Yet, they managed to stay in perfect harmony.

Everything started going well for Xander; even his parents noticed him smiling to himself here and there. This was a new phenomenon in their palace. It had been close to seven years since they had seen his smile, so they embraced the change with much enthusiasm. But alas, nothing really ever lasted in life. It had all been too good to be true.

The day she disappeared, Xander was the one to find her parents' dead with blood spewed out of their mouths as if they had been poisoned. He had felt the itch beneath his skin grow into a wildfire from the anger, grief, and fear he felt on the spot. He disintegrated the first person to touch him on the spot from all of his uncontrolled emotions. Then, he went home and cried his eyes out at the growing itch within him. The itch that told him she was gone. He knew she was not dead, regardless of what anyone said. He could not feel her anymore, but he knew, deep inside himself, he knew the bond was still there, hanging fragilely but ever present still. She was not dead, just gone. Maybe missing. He threw himself into his war classes, and instead of taking it easy, he toned up and gained skill.

When Serena's parents' advisor finally came to explain what transpired, he said Serena had killed her parents and run away with no explanation. But Xander knew. He just knew she was pure light. She would never do that. He used a lot of energy to not tear that advisor into shreds. He was, after all, the only family left for Serena. The anger drove him mad to the extent that he pushed himself hard in all of his training courses and graduated early. He went through the next motions silently and absentmindedly. He was crowned, graduated, and then volunteered to join all rescue missions for all kingdoms that opted to be Firgun's allies.

He eventually found himself at war; he would go for months fighting other people in the lands that did not belong to them and never felt the need to stop. Defending those who could not defend themselves, and he could feel all he wanted and not have to hold back. One of the teachers in his war and weaponry lecture had fashioned a weapon for him. As a way to reign him in, he had put a failsafe in it. The massive, large steel longsword was impressive and could slay dragons with one blow in the right direction. It channeled his magic straight from his depths. However, in order to keep him in check, every time he got carried away and tried to kill someone innocent or from his side, it only harmed them but gave him a deep identical cut that could not be healed except by light magic. The only person he ever wanted to heal him was the missing North Quadrant princess, Serena.

He had a deep, almost healed gash on his cheek that took four months to heal. He had other significant cuts on his back and torso. "Battle scars," he called them. They gave him a sense of purpose and direction. Every time he went to war, he tried to always come back without new ones. Sometimes he failed; sometimes he really tried and still failed. Instead, he began using his time to train and fight in wars, and he also tried to heal his marks alone. But the deep ache within his soul never left him. If anything, it made him feel as if he belonged. He was one with his magic, and in turn, one with the royal walls.

Some say that up to this day, when he gets angry, you can see tornados whirling in his eyes. Others say that once you see those thunderstorms, you are not leaving the battlefield alive.

～

Chamaine Kimbini is an avid reader who first discovered writing as a child. Writing showed her how wonderful the world is. Even while studying in medical school, writing was always a guilty pleasure of sorts, an escape and a familiar friend for which she always managed to make time. Through Wattpad, she learnt how to sharpen her skills and shape intricate worlds out of the simple words found in a dictionary. Letting people into her world, one punctuation mark after the other, is her passion. You can find her on Instagram: @the.unstable.bibliophile

A KID FROM THE EAST

MARK HEINZ

Winter, 1982

Michael pounded down the alley at nearly a full sprint, on the ragged edge of slipping on ice that was covered with only the thinnest layer of new snow. He'd been running for some time now, the muscles just above his knees burned. His throat felt raw, droplets of frozen saliva and snot dotted the right side of his face. It was just shy of 10 degrees below zero; actually the warmest it had been in more than a week.

The alley ran steeply between late 19th-century brick buildings. It was late afternoon, on the cusp of midwinter dusk with clear skies, so the light was flat and harsh.

He was headed downhill, which made footing all the more perilous, even for a twelve-year-old kid with exceptional agility.

Something whipped by the right side of his head, which was covered by a stocking cap and wrapped in the hood of his parka. His perception slowed nearly to a halt as it went past him far enough to come into full view. It was a rock, maybe half again as big as a golf ball. As its velocity slowed to more closely match his pace, it almost seemed to hang in the air in front of him. It made him think of ships in the Star Wars movies.

He started to slip. Just as his left hamstring tensed to compensate, something slammed into it.

Another rock, he surmised, even as his own barking grunt echoed in his head and his world began to turn sideways. He let out another grunt as he landed (fortunately, on the meaty part of his shoulder first) on his left side and then began sliding down the alley. For so long, he began to wonder if he'd stop before he shot out into the upcoming street.

When he stopped, he was still far enough up the alley that cars on the street wouldn't be a threat. Still, that also meant he was too far away to plead for help from any of the drivers.

The cars just continued to pass, going both ways, with their tires producing that weird, growling shriek that vulcanized rubber makes on packed snow in subzero weather.

The pain of the impact on his hamstring closed in just at the same time the kids who were chasing him did.

There were three of them. As Michael tried to rise, the first one let loose a kick that caught him in the face. He swore he could taste bits of sidewalk salt that had gotten caught in the tread of the kid's boot.

Michael tried to swing back, and managed to get to his knees when the second kid punched him in the ribs, which put him flat on his back. Pain now reigned supreme. He couldn't move or breathe. He could barely hear – only enough to catch the words "bastard" coming from one of his attackers.

One of them (the one who had kicked him, maybe) leaned over until his face was near Michael's. His breath was horrible – Michael could make out pickles and beer, he thought.

"Get up and fight, pussy!"

The wind came back into Michael's lungs with a rush, made excruciating by the frigid air.

"I will, if…" he started to say, weakly.

"If what, maggot?"

Michael grunted a couple more times, and his voice came back to about half normal strength.

"If you let me fight you alone, Gus. You prick."

Gus kicked him again, this time in the chest, knocking him flat. He leaned over again, bringing his face mere inches from Michael's. He had just inhaled in preparation to scream something else, when a baffled look took over his face and he began to straighten back up.

This allowed Michael enough of a break to push himself up onto his elbows, affording him a view past Gus to his two buddies, Stephen and Jake.

A weird, off-pitch sound, almost like the call of some bizarre bird, came from behind him. Before he had time to ponder it further, a figure darting in at amazing speed leapt past him and Gus, and landed clumsily in front of the other two.

It was a scrawny kid.

Still trying to gather his wits, Michael made out that he was wearing a seemingly impossible combination of one of those leather, fur-lined over-the-ears caps (he thought, like a World War Two bomber pilot, maybe?), a trench coat, some sort of ratty pants, red mittens and… moon boots.

Puzzled up until that point, Michael was stunned when the scrawny kid slapped Stephen across the face and then began to evade retaliation by dancing around like a demented puppet without strings. He began shouting "Ya! Ya!" and whistling through his teeth at intervals, like a rancher driving cattle.

Not long into this spectacle, Jake made a lunge at the newcomer but slipped on the ice and tumbled onto his side.

The scrawny kid began cackling and took another swipe at Stephen, who dodged it, but then lost his balance and fell on his ass.

Their tormentor threw his head back and started what might have been a howl, but he too slipped and fell, ending up on his knees, and began laughing hysterically.

By this time Gus had straightened up, and Michael was attempting to stand, but his bafflement gave way to pain, and he sank back down to his elbows.

Then, thundering over the scrawny kid's laughter, there was another voice. It was also a kid's, but it carried authority.

"Three on one? Makes you nothin' but a puss, Gus!"

Michael cranked his head around to see a boy about his age coming up the alley. He was blocky and spooky-strong looking. He had a crew cut; Michael could see this because, despite the frigid temperature, he wasn't wearing a hat. He only wore a ranch-style fleece-lined Levi's jacket, leather gloves, jeans, and tennis shoes.

Looking genuinely concerned, Gus stepped off to Michael's right and grimly took a fighting stance.

This new kid didn't even break his stride as he closed the gap, smoothly brought up his right arm and drilled Gus square in the face.

Gus didn't make a sound. He went straight down onto his ass and stayed there, blinking as his nose bled.

"You two, stay down!" the blocky kid roared. Michael cranked his gaze back up the alley, just in time to see the scrawny kid, still cackling, make it to his feet and start brushing himself off.

Stephen and Jake complied.

Crew cut turned to Michael.

"You OK, there, Champ?"

Michael nodded and grunted as he managed to slowly stand back up.

"I'm Dave. Can you walk?"

Michael nodded again. He and Dave started walking back toward the street, shoulder-to-shoulder, with Michael limping.

Just as they got to the end of the alley, Dave turned back around, and his face turned angry.

"Jesus Christ, Robby!" he bellowed.

Michael turned back to look.

Robby was standing over Gus from behind. He'd taken his mittens off and was starting to work his fly, as if he intended to whip it out and whizz on Gus' head.

"C'mon, let's just go," Dave said, slightly less angrily.

Robby hastily pulled his mittens back on and again broke into laughter as he galloped down the remainder of the alley to meet them.

* * *

Michael stood in front of the candy bar section, the second of four considerably narrow aisles in the cramped but pleasant Mom and Pop neighborhood store, called Nicky's. It was an exactly square structure with an interior space probably not more than 400 square feet (and that was counting the storeroom and cooler in the back.) The exterior was a plain but not unpleasant shade of brown; it sat on a street otherwise occupied by modest working-class homes, most of which had been built between the 1920s and 1950s.

Nicky's had been there since the 1930s. Nobody was sure who the namesake was, but the owner and generally sole operator—the ironically named Eugene McCarthy—looked old enough to have been there from the beginning.

He was relaxing in a small chair behind the cash register, reading a bass fishing magazine. Which was a bit odd, the nearest bass fishing was hundreds of miles away, and as far as anybody knew, Mr. McCarthy never left town. He lived alone in a house, decidedly small even for that neighborhood, just a couple doors down from the store.

Dave approached the register with a fistful of Smarties candy, his personal favorite. Robby was pacing about, humming to himself and pulling on a bottle of Mountain Dew, which he would empty before he got to the register to pay for it.

Michael was trying to decide between a Milky Way and a Snickers. He was grimacing — partly because of the quandary but also because of his various pains, which by now were thudding dully.

The boys had stopped in here after walking nearly a mile from the heart of downtown, where the alley fight had occurred. They'd stopped in just as much to get a break from the cold as to score some sweets. Their homes were still several blocks away; Michael's was the farthest away. During the walk, they'd chatted as boys getting to know each other do: about their favorite movies, TV shows or movies, and a budding interest in girls. Dave, usually rather stoic, had brightened up when the subject of AC/DC came up. He'd already memorized most of the lyrics on this year's "Flick of the Switch" album.

Michael finally settled on a Snickers, and he and Robby went to the register together before meeting Dave by the door. They lingered there for a bit, with Robby standing between the other two, steeling themselves against the cold. It was nearly sundown now, so the day's already frigid temperatures had dropped considerably.

Mr. McCarthy had gone back to his magazine after ringing Robby and Michael through. He looked up at the boys, whose backs were now turned to him, and smiled.

"Now, Dave, I know you're a native son and tough as nails, but I think it's gotten cold enough, even you need a hat," he said. "I've got a spare here. You want it?"

Dave turned to face him.

"Oh, thanks, Mr. McCarthy, but I've got one stashed in my pocket."

"Well, then put it on, you damn loon," the elderly man said with a chuckle before starting to read again.

Dave pulled a blue military-style cold weather watch cap out of his right coat pocket but didn't put it on quite yet.

"You know, this can be a tough place to be the new kid," he said to Michael, finally broaching the subject of what had brought them together. "Not many people move here, 'specially since the mine slowed down. Everybody's kind of set."

"And you're different," piped Robby, who really didn't have much of a filter.

"I know," Michael said. "My parents are, yeah, like, important people, and we have money, and we're from New Hampshire, so everybody thinks me and my little sister are some kind of spoiled snobs. But I can be a regular guy, you know? Nice, like you guys."

"Yeah," Dave said. "You just gotta let people get to know that, and to hell with the ones who don't figure it out. Gonna be hard; back East isn't looked at too kindly here."

"Yeah!" said Robby, practically shouting.

Mr. McCarthy didn't look up. He was used to Robby.

"Like my Dad says, 'Fat kids from back East!'" Robby blurted and clapped Michael on the back.

Michael grunted with a fresh wave of pain.

He socked Robby in his left shoulder. Robby started laughing again, and the other two chuckled as Dave pulled on his cap and they stepped through the door. Clouds of frosty breath engulfed them as Mr. McCarthy watched them leave, and then he rose to go about closing the store.

❧

Mark Heinz has extensive experience with print publications dating back to the late 1980s. After graduating from the College of Journalism at the University of Montana (Missoula), he landed his first job as a reporter in Dillon, Montana and went on to work for several newspapers and magazines across the Mountain West. He also edited or helped re-write several non-fiction books and coached writers, novice and seasoned. Likening the pace, pressure, and exacting standards of newsrooms to "the Marine Corps for writers," Mark believes in combining the no-nonsense approach of the editors he came up under with constructive guidance toward the goal of improving and refining the author's voice.

THE SKY DRINKER
NAHAL NAIB

The shimmery ink glinted across the surface of the rocky walls. Fourteen-year-old Dove snuck into her hideout to vent her feelings for another night, risking her safety once more.

6/3/19

>   *I went to the hospital this morning to see Aaron. I have to say he's making rapid progress—toward death. Since yesterday, he was in a coma, and today the doctors told us he won't make it. I don't know what to think or how to hope when I know there's no point. All I can say is that he was a good friend.*

The cursive words floating in front of her eyes made her stomach turn. She saw Aaron's smiling face flash across her mind and fade away just as quickly as it appeared. Aaron was no more in this world.

It had been one whole week since the massive earthquake hit Air-Dome; the earthquake that killed Aaron. Dove felt like a deceiver coming back to The Forbidden Hill after such a terrible accident.

Dove grasped her golden felt-tip pen tighter in her hand and uncapped it, the ink ready to ooze out. She heaved a sigh and held it in front of herself, right below the last entry which was on the day her partner-in-crime left without even saying goodbye. She thought it was funny how she called him the deceiver as her initial reaction to his death when she was the one deceiving everyone right now.

6/10/19

> *It's been an entire week now. Aaron Royce is dead, and I don't feel anything. The world lost another piece of itself, but why don't I feel empty? It's sad what happened, and I'm sure a boy as nice as him didn't deserve it, but I'm not crying like the thousands of other people to whom he was dear. I could never forget the sight of him struggling to run faster than the landslide. But it caught up to him. I couldn't do anything.*

The last drops of dark blue fluid squirted out and formed big blobs, staining the invisible page upon which her words were suspended. Dove tapped her thumb on the bottom of the pen, but the ink had finished. She shook her head disappointedly and sat down on a boulder near the cave opening.

Even though there was nothing left to do, Dove didn't feel like going back home. She looked up at the stars that twinkled on the vast indigo blanket and wondered if her friend was happy up there. His battle was over, but he left so many people at emotional war with themselves.

She popped the lid of the felt-tipped pen and turned it face-down, as if making it drink from a pot of normal ink. Even after years of practicing the same ritual of feeding the Sky to her pen, Dove was mesmerised every time by the fact that the sky, which was made of nothing, turned itself into a fluid and entered the nib. She remembered what her grandmother said to her two years ago: *The Sky Drinker was a gift to her grandfather from an old magician king; it was her responsibility to keep the existence of such a thing a secret from everyone.*

* * *

Waiting for her device to charge, she leaned back on the rough wall behind her and closed her eyes, letting out a deep exasperated breath. When her eyes opened next, the sun was peeking out from the horizon, minutes from rising. Dove gasped, immediately realizing the importance of heading back before anyone found out she was missing.

Putting the lid back on, Dove scrambled to her feet and rushed down, her legs stiff. Before leaving, she closed the mouth of the cave with the boulder she was sitting on, sealing away all her secrets and deepest feelings. If the mountain crumbled down to dust any time soon, as the people of Air-Dome feared, her most precious words would be buried under the rubble, just as Aaron had been. At least those words would stay there forever.

A few days later, as the town began to settle down after the loss, the deep tremors of the Earth were back. But unlike last time, Dove wasn't afraid of what was to come. Despite her better judgment, she kept returning to the hill and continued visiting the cave that she had claimed as her own. The series of mini-earthquakes hadn't stopped for several days, and the experts said a major one was on its way. She hardly cared.

Dove slid the Sky Drinker into her rucksack and pulled open her window; a gush of cool air slapped her face. She looked over her shoulder before hauling herself onto the road. On the way, she told herself this was the last time she was taking this risk. She didn't want an ending like Aaron's, but she wasn't willing to say goodbye to her favorite place in the world.

As she tiptoed past the barrier and took a turn into the danger zone, her heart skipped a beat. From the corner of her eye she spotted a ray of white light heading her way. She picked up her pace, careful to remain silent, but twigs snapped under her feet, causing her to wince.

"Hey! Who's there?" somebody called; it was a familiar voice echoing in the silence of the night.

"*Dad?*" she whispered to herself, crouching down further behind the bush. She was frightened all of a sudden. She hoped he hadn't seen her and that he'd just walk away without investigating, but he continued walking towards the bush.

He peered over, and she had no choice but to reveal herself. She emerged out of the bush and faced him, ready to take the chiding.

"You know you could have died tonight, don't you?" he asked after a few moments of silence, his volume higher than usual and harsher than ever.

"I know," she mumbled.

"Dove, I'm very disappointed in you," he said, pointing the flashlight to the ground.

There was no response.

"How long have you been doing this?" he demanded, his voice hoarse.

"A few days," she lied. Her instincts always told her to save herself first and think later. The least she could do was tell the truth and get this over with. The burden of a deceased friend was enough.

"No, tell the truth," he said, seeing through her white lie.

She inhaled sharply, pulling herself together. "Okay, it's been a long time. I won't come here again," she said, desperate to get away from this situation.

But Mr McKeath wasn't willing to let this go so easily. "Were you there the day Aaron was injured?"

Dove was surprised by the question. She stared at him; she didn't need light to see the scornful look on his face.

"I'm asking you something," he persisted.

Dove pursed her lips. She gathered all her courage and asked him a question he wasn't able to answer. "What about the times I've seen you here?"

"What?"

"I'm not the only one who's risked her life-"

"You're right. Aaron used to fool around with his life too, and look where that got him," he said, interrupting her.

Dove shook her head in disbelief "Why do *you* come here?" She asked fiercely, ignoring his remark about Aaron.

Instead of answering her, he said, "You're grounded. For two months." Then he started making his way in the other direction. "Come on, let's get you home."

Dove was frustrated. "You can't ground me," she said helplessly.

He didn't say anything, didn't even stop to see if she was following.

"*Dad!*" Dove yelled. "Dad, stop! You can't ground me. My whole life is here—" She caught her breath, conscious of what she had just disclosed.

He turned around and walked toward her. "Do you have any idea how risky this is? Aaron lost his life because of this foolishness-"

"It's not foolishness," she said defensively. "Don't call Aaron a fool. He was brave, that's what he was."

There was a low grumble beneath their feet. The two went silent. "Oh no," she whispered and before she knew it Mr McKeath was hurrying her to the car that was parked nearby. The tremors got wilder and wilder with every step. A huge boulder tumbled down and crashed near the wheels of the car, right in the spot where Dove had been standing a few moments ago. She screamed in horror.

They drove home and took refuge in their rooms while the Earth continued shaking. Dove held on to the windowsill, her heart pounding. She thought about what her father told her in the car, "It could have been you this time."

On her way to the local theme park two months later, when her punishment was over, Dove thought about her grandparents and the word she'd given to them, but she also remembered the note that just happened to fall out of a drawer when the furniture rocked about during the quake. She wondered why she had never read it before.

> *The words you write will dissolve back into the sky where they came from as soon as the Sky Drinker is destroyed. And when the knowledge of its existence is in danger, it's better for it to be wiped off the face of the world.*
>   *P.S:- Your father knows.*

* * *

Whilst ascending the Ferris wheel, she considered climbing back down many times. It was way past midnight and the town was asleep, which meant nobody could come to her rescue if something went wrong. Finally, on reaching the seat at the very top, she glanced down; she'd climbed a tremendous height above the ground and it made her nauseous, but there was no backing down now.

Mustering up all the courage inside herself, she got up to her feet and raised the pen to the sky.

> *Dear Dad,*
>   *I know I've been a very disobedient daughter lately, and I'm sorry for that. This hill has been like a second home to me, and it's*

*sure going to be hard to say goodbye. But now that I realize the fear
you have of losing me, I've come back to my senses.*
Love,
Your daughter

She carefully lowered herself and sat down. She glanced at the pen, and with a heavy heart lifted it above her head, ready to fling it away as far as she could see. But then she stopped.

"Somebody else will find it," she said to herself. Thinking of a better alternative, she descended to the ground.

Mr. McKeath was watching from the window of his room. His mouth was set in a warm smile as he squinted to make out the glittery cursive handwriting.

"She's such a daredevil," he said softly, shaking his head. He pulled a pen from his pocket and his smile grew wider.

Pulling his window open, he stepped out and fled into the night.

∽

Nahal Naib lives in Karachi with her three younger siblings and parents. She developed an interest in writing at the age of 12 and began posting her work on Wattpad in 2016 @KrazyKupKake1234. She is doing her A levels in English Literature, Psychology, and Business Studies. She is also part of the Publications Society in her school and is working to hone her skills as an aspiring author. You can follow her on Instagram @Nahalwrites for daily tips and advice on how to deal with things most of us are struggling with, including stress and bullying.

Witness for the Forgotten

Lydia M. Reaves

The house sighs with old age, *leave me alone*. My eyes can't avert their gaze. I've loved this place far too long to walk away now, not when I finally have the opportunity to investigate further. There is a stout iron gate that guards the house and keeps it company. Through the overgrown weeds, I peer at its beauty and decipher a path to its front door.

I'm not sure why no one inherited the poor old house. Maybe the old couple that lived here didn't have a family? It's a shame really; this house would've made a perfect home. I reach through the bars and pick the lock using a couple of bent bobby pins. Click, click, CLICK. Slipping through the gate by the light of the full moon, I make my way, wading through the weeds to the grand entrance.

I can see the way the years have chipped away at this place with wrinkles like those on an old woman's face. Even in her elderly state, she composes herself as I draw closer. She is excited by the promise of companionship. Though her siding is a dull, dejected gray, she winks at me to come closer. Vines grow up her sides and take the porch over, like black smoke circling and rising. The porch floor is littered with what look like old soiled envelopes, covered in grime and mildew. The front door almost seems new, besides the sun-bleached what used-to-be-dark hardwood. The door flaunts stained glass with gold trim. The glass seems to wink at me in the moonlight, *come on in.*

It isn't locked. The dust that had settled on everything stirs when the door creeks open. The moonlight creeps in from the back and illuminates everything in a blue haze. The dust in the air seems to sparkle, *welcome*. I let my eyes adjust to the minimal light. The house is decaying from the outside in, but the elements haven't had their field day inside yet. It's dusty and dark, and there are creepy crawlies in the cool dark corners, but it's here, a testimony to its strength and endurance. It's ancient but not decrepit, not useless.

Remaining where I am by the door, I notice a formal living room with the furniture still there, covered with layers of dust and grime. I can imagine a family sitting there, enjoying the sunset through the bay window. I see an old-fashioned radio and squeal inwardly with excitement. The dining room is set and ready to feed an army. The tarnished silver cutlery is lying peacefully next to the ornately hand-painted porcelain on the heavy oak table.

The artwork somewhat similar to my painting style—thick broad strokes in richly colored paint—covers the walls. There is one landscape in particular that I take a moment to indulge in. The sky is a vibrant shade of purple, the mountains are a deep blue, and the trees glow green and pale yellow. I get sucked in and stare a moment longer than I should. I smile; how beautiful. Then my eyebrows crease; it is a very modern-looking painting. Why is it here?

I notice on the ground next to me yet another envelope. This one was shielded from the elements, so it only has a bit of dust. I pick it up: empty, so I place it gently back where I found it. That's odd. My face forms a confused frown, but I quickly put it out of my mind so I can direct my attention to the main event.

The entrance certainly is grand. The staircase swivels and dances in front of me, *look at me. You know I'm beautiful.* And it is. The handrail feels like butter as I slide my hand up, up, up; I let the rail guide me up the stairs. I wipe the collected dust off my hand as I move slowly through the house, so as to disturb it as little as possible.

The hardwood floor complains in a shrill voice, *be gentle! I'm old.* I try my best to tread lightly. I wish I could apologize to it. I wander through the house and analyze each room as I go. The hall directs me, shows me the way, leads me. *Start here.* There is a bedroom with a twin-sized bed against the far wall, just opposite the door. It welcomes me, *come have a look*. It would be rude to refuse, so I take a gentle step in and give it a respectful once-over.

The wallpaper is quaint, with little white horses on a light pink background. There is a charming little desk with a white chair to match in the corner next to the closet. Amateur paintings line the walls. If it weren't for the dust, this would make a lovely room for a little girl. I see a rather large spider scuttle on the rose-colored rug, so I take my leave on to the next.

It's a classic library with shelves that go up to the ceiling. All the books I wish I had are here, all my favorites. I take a moment and allow myself to relish the feel of the spines of the old books in my hands. The smell is so familiar from the musty, well-loved books. Some of them look like they've been read a hundred times. If they were mine, I certainly would.

I gingerly place the books back on the wooden shelves to turn my attention to the center of the space, where a mahogany desk lies. What a cool desk! I've always wanted one. Heavy and warm, it grounds the room and adds a significance to the house. *I'm important.*

I peer at the desk and notice a photo. There's a man with dark features, short thick eyebrows that have a bit of a bend to them. His eyes seem kind; his smile is small but fills the photo. His arm is wrapped around a girl, about seven or eight. Her features are lighter, but she has the same smile, and their ears pop out and play peek-a-boo the same way. It has to be her father.

I think of my own father, and I wonder what he'd think of me now wandering through this abandoned house on a whim. He probably wouldn't like it much. "Lila, what are you doing? You aren't a child anymore. Quit acting like you were born yesterday."

But he's not here, so I drown out the sound of his voice and try not to think of the last night I saw my parents. I wipe a tear from my face, *remember*. I need to focus on the task at hand. Now is not the time. I concentrate on my steps as I exit the library.

I stride past the bathroom; it can't possibly offer anything of value other than spiders, which I do not have a particular fondness for. I feel a shiver down my spine at the thought. I press on and find a larger room —a light shade of blue coats the walls. Two large windows let in more light than in the other rooms. There are several pieces of mahogany furniture, two chests of drawers, a vanity with an ornate rose-etched mirror, and a bench with gold fabric at the foot of the bed. In all class and style, the bed is, of course, a canopy. Gold translucent fabric hangs from the mahogany frame. I wish I could have a room like this. I've always wanted a canopy bed, such a romantic notion.

One of the pictures on the bedside table seems interesting, *look over here*. It's the same man as before, this time in a tux: his wedding day. His face seems to light up with joy as he looks at his bride. She is wearing an elegant dress, complete with full sleeves of lace. I do a double-take and almost drop the frame when my eyes meet hers. I almost don't recognize her without mascara, and I've never seen her smile that wide. She is me. Her rosy lips, her dirty blonde hair, her slender face. That's me. It's like I'm looking in a mirror.

What? I'm not married. I don't even know that man, but here I am looking at a picture of my wedding day. It's already happened. Is this a joke? Was this Photoshopped? I strip the frame from the photo; I desperately claw at the little metal tabs on the back. I throw the empty frame to the ground and hear the glass shatter on the hardwood floor. I hold the photo in my hand and on the back is an inscription that I have to read twice:

To my love,
May we always cherish each other like we did on that day.
Happy 10th! XOXO Lila

This time I do drop the photo to the ground. It's my handwriting. I wrote it. But I haven't yet. But it's done. It's here. It's mine.

Despite the layers of dust and the smell of mildew, I can't help but sit on the bed. My legs buckle and bend beneath me. I can feel my heart pumping in my chest; I can hear the rushing of my blood in my ears. I sit. I stare at the photo resting on the floor; I stare into my eyes, and I sit with my mouth wide open. It's the life I've always wanted: the house, the man, the kid. But it feels strange to receive it out of order. Do I get to be happy one day? Is this my future?

I'm not sure how long I sit there. Perhaps a minute, perhaps an hour. What is the difference?

I notice, wedged in the corner of the frame, a piece of paper and, despite my heartbeat ringing in my ears, I can't help but take a look. I kneel to the floor and reach for the paper. Again in my handwriting:

Lila,

> *Don't be frightened. Everything is going to be fine. Something amazing is about to happen.*
Lila

I hear a loud, distinct knock at the door. My eyes widen, and my chest feels tight. What now? Should I get up? Should I stay on the bed? Someone knows I'm here. I suppose avoiding them won't do any good.

Still, I find it hard to put weight on my wobbly legs. After a few moments, I stand and slowly walk back out of the room. I trek past the bathroom, past the library, past the little girls' room, and down the stairs. Down. Down. Down.

Once filled with a warm glow, my whole body now feels cold as I reach for the doorknob. I muster a whisper. "Who's there?"

Silence.

I am breathing heavily now. My chest is thumping, and my body is aching as my hand feels the cool touch of the knob. Usually, I run warm, and I would take a second to enjoy the relief, but now I only hesitate from fear. "Who's there." Not a question. Shaky, but louder than before.

No answer.

I wait for another moment.

Nothing. It takes all of my strength to turn the knob and open the door.

"Who's there?!" This time desperate yelling.

My voice, my hands, my legs: shaking. I step out and turn my head quickly to check both sides of the porch. No one. Did I imagine the knocking? Was it all in my head?

Eyes tightly closed, I hang my head in my hands and take a deep breath. I steady my breathing and settle my heartbeat. My gaze focuses on the ground. By my feet is something curious—an envelope. A plain white envelope, like what I saw before, only this one is new; it's sealed.

I pick it up. It's blank, with no name and no address. Nothing. I pace for a moment and find myself amongst the weeds. After a bit of hesitation, I carefully rip the side of the envelope to reveal what's inside.

A card. An intricate gold-pressed card with swirls and roses. I run my fingers over the foil and feel the detail, like raised bubbles on a page. I open it, expecting to see something remotely frightening staring back at me.

Nothing. It's blank. I shake my head. What a prank! Who planned this? Maybe Rebecca. She's always looking for ways to cheer me up.

I smile. "Rebecca!"

I look up, and I'm not where I was. The smirk is wiped off my face. Or rather, I'm in the same place, but I hardly recognize it. The sunshine beams down on the manicured lawn, and each blade of grass is in place. There's not a weed in sight. Disoriented, I spin around to look at the porch. It's pristine, complete with a bench swing and rocking chairs.

The house! The house is as good as new. It's even better in this restored glory. The paint is a vibrant shade of blue, and the siding is in perfect condition. The windows wink, *hey there, stranger.* In my stupor, my elation, my confusion, I drop the card. It hits the stone pathway with a gentle thud.

I bring my gaze down to the man in the doorway. I recognize him as the same one from the pictures. His eyes are soft. He's been expecting me.

"Hello...?" I'm hesitant.

He is sure. "Hello, my love."

∾

Lydia Reaves is a short story writer with a couple of novels in the works. Her work "Witness for the Forgotten" is her first published piece. Lydia has a podcast, "Books and Other Things I Love," where she talks about things relating to her love of books and writing. Other than her podcast, the best place to get to know her is on Instagram @Lydia.m.reaves. If you'd like to read more of her work, her short stories are available on her website, www.Lydiamreaves.com.

Section Two:

Unrequited Love

UnRestrained
By Linne Elizabeth

Unpretentious, that's how Collin wanted to appear. He adjusted the collar on his maroon Apartment 9 button-up to keep it from rubbing a sensitive spot on his neck. The shirt, a far cry from his usual Armani, was a new look for a new man. One unfortunate side effect: the cheap fabric lacked the strength to withstand his nerves. Sweat began to bleed through the cotton poly blend. If he didn't get a grip, his anxiety would be visible beneath his arms.

He drummed his fingers on the black tablecloth draped over a circular table for two. His emotions were getting the better of him. It had been so long since he'd seen Jennifer in person. She wouldn't recognize him now. She couldn't. Not with all the procedures he'd undergone to make this date a reality.

Two years ago, Collin hadn't existed. He was Mark. Mark and Jennifer were happy and in love. One day he dreamed of placing a large diamond on her finger, buying her a house, and having two kids; instead his fantasy dissolved like salt in his buttery noodles during their final meal together.

"You're just too controlling. I can't breathe." She placed a hand on her chest to emphasize the point.

"Controlling?" The word tasted sour and wrong.

"Yes! You won't let me go anywhere alone. Every time I turn around, you're there."

Dangerous people filled the world. Jennifer was his precious jewel: intelligent, funny, and sexy as hell. She needed protection, and he wanted to keep her safe. She didn't see it that way. She felt imprisoned. That was her word, *imprisoned.* She used an allegory of a caged bird who needed to be set free before she slammed the door to his brownstone apartment.

He cursed himself for not being a better boyfriend. Jennifer deserved the world, so he tried to make things right. After many failed text attempts and one nasty run in at the gym where she trained, she got a restraining order.

A restraining order! He scoffed.

The couple at the neighboring table looked in his direction. His face flushed with heat, and he avoided their eyes by pretending to examine the clear salt and pepper shakers. He checked his Rolex, a single relic from his past life. She was late. Not her usual style. Her punctuality stood out as one of her best qualities. That and her smile.

When she smiled, her supple lips parted wide for a view of pearl white teeth, almost perfect except for a small chip in one of her front teeth. An imperfection that made her human and endearing. That chip served as a reminder of her frailty and her inability to take care of herself. That was why he violated the restraining order. The guy outside the deli wanted more than to hand her a dollar she dropped.

Collin didn't regret punching the guy, but he hated being separated from Jennifer. Not knowing where she was or who she was with kept him awake most nights. A recurring nightmare of her lying in a ditch caused him to scream out in the middle of the night on more than one occasion. His cellmate was always happy to silence him with a solid punch to the gut. The physical pain was second only to the emotional turmoil of being away from her.

He did not have many resources while incarcerated, but he had time. Time and a library. He spent days immersed in magazines, books, articles, anything that would set him on a track to secure his love in his arms again. In two months, he'd devoured the limited book selection. At a loss for how he'd win Jennifer back, he meandered the yard where he overheard two older men:

"The doctor botched it."

"Serves him right for finding some low-life hack in Brick City."

"His face looked like a cheesesteak."

"I'd shell for the real deal."

"Plastic surgery ain't cheap."

Plastic surgery! Why had he never considered it? He had a bottomless inheritance that he had planned to spend on Jennifer. Perhaps a nice house in the Jersey suburbs where she'd be protected from the dangers of the city. Now he'd use his money to win her back. Then he'd spend the rest of his life spoiling her.

With time served, he started the arduous process to transform himself into a man Jennifer would want to be with again. The first steps were easy, distancing himself from family and known associates, changing his name. Collin emerged from an excessive amount of money and a sharp blade. It was a year of augmentation, implants, and too many -plasties to remember. Mark no longer existed. Collin would be a man Jennifer wouldn't recognize and couldn't refuse.

"Excuse me, sir. Can I get you something to drink?" A man in a white tuxedo shirt that stretched over his broad chest stood by the small table.

Envy for the waiter's pecs tore through Collin. Maybe he could fit in one more procedure before things got serious with Jennifer. Collin shook his head. "Thank you, but I'll wait."

The waiter nodded his head. "Would you like a breadbasket?"

Collin nodded. Bread seemed fitting. Bagels were how this whole second chance came about.

He was eager to meet up with her again, but it took time to find her. He scoured dating profiles and struck gold with Jdate. She was unattached. He wouldn't need to deal with another man like the one outside the deli. He messaged her and let the romance begin anew.

That first message had been thrilling. His heart thundered, sending rushes of adrenaline through his body. He was one step closer to being with her again. The first message had to be something simple. Understated. Something that would make her melt without tipping her off. One slip-up, and she'd be gone forever.

Scrolling to her hobbies, he saw it. The way back into her life practically jumped off the screen: "Connoisseur of Bagels." His fingers flew across the keyboard. "As a bagel enthusiast, you must know the best place in town. Where should a newcomer go first?"

That simple question set off a volley of messages. Her tinkling soprano voice filled his mind when he read her responses. Each notification of a new message was like surfacing after a deep dive he didn't know he'd made. He felt renewed and energized by her attention. It took only two weeks of near constant messages before she suggested they meet IRL.

So, here he sat, planted at a table for two at the Ristorante Italia, a mid-price restaurant with low lighting and an exquisite bruschetta. He rubbed his palms on his slacks. If this went wrong, it was over; twenty procedures and months of recovery to return to square one.

Jennifer breezed through the doorway; her five-foot eleven-inch frame wrapped in an emerald cocktail dress that highlighted her curvy figure. She scanned the crowd, and her mocha eyes lit with recognition when she met his gaze. His heart hammered creating a steady drumming in his ears.

This was the moment that would define the past two years.

Collin stood, pushing back his chair, and waved once at her. She weaved through the tables to greet him with a bright smile and a quick embrace.

"It's nice to meet you in person." She gazed at him through thick eyelashes.

Collin relaxed. She didn't recognize him. Hallelujah! He wanted to pick her up and swing her around. Instead, he cupped her hand and brought it to his lips. With a feather-soft kiss on the back of her hand, he said, "I couldn't agree more."

∾

Linne Elizabeth is an award-winning author and ardent defender of the Oxford comma. She somehow finds time to read 50-plus novels a year while raising four (sometimes feral) kids. When she's not feeding or ferrying her kids to activities, you might find her hiding in her closet devouring chocolate chips while developing gripping plot lines for future projects. When she's really lucky, she gets to escape on adventures with her supportive husband, who doesn't mind that she brings a library along with her. (Thank heavens for Kindle.)

ECHOES

KATE SEGER

I remember the way sunlight splashed across his face, dappling it with shadow. We met in this forest, amid the stands of fir and pine that have swathed Mount Kithairon since the dawn of days. This vale is my home and my captivity for eternity; the realm to which Hera banished me for my "lust."

After she stole my words, of course.

Never mind that it was Zeus who forced himself upon me, who cajoled and wheedled his way into my arms and my heart. I was an Oread. Treacherous seduction was bred into my immortal blood. Who would believe that I was not to blame?

Certainly not Hera.

If Zeus was my first mistake, Narcissus was my greatest. I should have known better than to reveal myself to a mortal. That was reckless. Did I really believe that Hera and the Fates would allow me to be happy?

I was a fool.

But this is how it all began.

The mortal stalked my forest, sleek, sinuous, and feline. I followed him for days before I dared approach. Silently I prowled, keeping my lithe body reed thin, pressing against the trunks of the trees, trusting them to keep me hidden. I watched by night as he stretched out his sculpted body and rested in the glow of his campfire. I watched by day, when he was at his loveliest. It was summer, and he was often bare-chested, beads of sweat glistening on his breast.

I was drawn to him. And like a fool, I threw caution to the wind.

He was standing in a small clearing, bow held aloft. His arrow was sighted on a whitetail gazelle, one eye squinting, the other bright and blue as a mountain pool. His skin was golden in the afternoon light, a tangle of sandy blonde hair windswept away from his face.

I wanted him to see me, to know me, to love me.

That is the nature of an Oread, after all, or so I've been told: to long for and to yearn to be longed for.

It is also, I believe, the nature of love.

I stepped out from behind the sheltering arms of a great sentinel tree. The intentional rustle of brush drew the mortal's eye and distracted him long enough for the doe to bound off gracefully through the underbrush.

At first his finely chiseled face was carved into a mask of irritation, his eyes narrowed, aquiline nose held high aloft, jaw clenched. Then, slowly, he recognized me for what I was.

I should tell you, I am no great beauty amongst the gods. I have seen Aphrodite with her golden flowing locks, rosebud lips, and pearlescent skin emanating seduction like a beacon. That is not me. I am only a mountain nymph, a small goddess. But I have wiles of my own, and to a mortal who has never before seen a goddess, I am not without my charms.

"Greetings," he finally said. His voice was warm. His gaze turned admiring as it roved over my body. I gnawed my lower lip, feeling uncomfortable with my nakedness on full display. It had been so long since I had consorted with a mortal. I felt feral in his presence.

"Greetings," I mimicked back. My voice was a flat breathy thing. I winced at the sound of it. I, who used to lure men into my arms with a song, now had no words of my own.

"I hope I do not trespass upon your forest, lady?" he asked smoothly, eyebrow arching.

"Forest," I murmured, a flush creeping into my cheeks. I smiled weakly, hoping to appear welcoming. I prayed that I didn't look quite the fool I felt. Trembling, I took a few small steps closer. I tapped myself on the chest.

"Echo." I steeled myself and spoke the one word of my own that Hera had left me—my name. Hearing it upon my own lips, I felt a flicker of the girl

I had once been rekindle. I struck what I hoped was an alluring pose. I was, after all, a nymph. Seduction was in my blood. If I wanted this mortal, I would have him.

"Narcissus," he returned. My smile began to feel a bit more natural.

I beckoned. His lips quirked up, amused. He moved towards me with long confident strides. He opened his mouth to speak, but I drew a finger to my lips. I would have him silent, like me. I took his large, calloused, hands in mine. I drew them first to my lips, kissing each knuckle, and then I placed them on my shoulders.

He understood.

He traced my collar bone, skimming fingers over my breasts, circling my navel, then planting his hands firmly on my hips. There was hunger in his eyes. I drew my tongue slowly over my lips.

He drew me down onto the pine needle carpet of the forest floor, and he took me.

Perhaps it was a kind of revenge. Zeus had ravaged me, tricked and deceived me, and then left me to Hera's mercy. Yet after all those long years, I still had some small power of my own.

Afterwards, we lay in the twilight; my body curled against his as the sky shifted from bright scarlet to the purple of a bruise. He whispered endearments into my ear and curled long tendrils of my hair around his fingers. When we awoke, the sun was high in the sky, but it was a softer, gentler sun—as if Helios had chosen to take pity on me as I lay in this young mortal's embrace.

So it was that he came to spend a season in my forest, and we walked the woodland trails side by side. I showed him the hidden places where waterfalls caught the light just so, forming majestic rainbows, and the dens where fox pups tumbled with one another. Narcissus chattered endlessly. I could only respond in clipped mimicry, but I listened to his every word. He spoke only of himself. His name was Narcissus. I did not mind. I had lived so long in a world without words that each one was like a drop of water after years of drought.

I wanted him to stay forever. I knew that he could not. Even if things had been different, he was a mortal. His bright beauty was destined to fade. But I, headstrong and happy, refused to think about that.

I cannot say how long we shared this enchanted forest. Time moves differently in the realm of the gods. It was long enough that I grew to know and cherish his every expression. The way his jaw muscle twitched when he concentrated, how his smile spread slowly and lazily across his face. The only place I dared not bring him was my pool. I knew Hera had placed a heavy enchantment upon that spot. I did not know the nature of the foul spell she had cast and did not wish to know. Whenever Narcissus drew near it, I would tug on his arm and lead him away.

Then one day, when the leaves had changed to red and gold, I awoke to find him gone. The autumn air was cold, and the north wind hissed in my ears, lashing me with his tongue. I waited for what felt like eternity, shivering and silently begging every god in Olympia to return my love to me.

But the gods had long been deaf to me.

How can one's pleas be heard when one does not have a voice?

I searched the forest until there was but one place left to look. Fear coiled in my belly as I dragged myself toward the enchanted pool. It was a secluded spot, deep in the woodlands. By now, Narcissus knew this forest nearly as well as I. Surely he'd noticed my trickery to keep him from the spot. I never imagined it would pique his curiosity, and he would venture there on his own.

I cursed Hera. If only I had my words, I could have warned him away, explained why we dare not enter that one glade.

I began to run, padding quickly across the rock strewn path, clumsy in my terror. Perhaps there was still time to sway him from this folly.

I bounded into the clearing where the river fanned out into a wide pool. Trees bowed their heads around the spot, casting shadows over the still waters. I breathed a sigh of relief when I saw him perched upon the bank, gazing calmly into the water as lily pads drifted by. Naive as I was, I thought he was safe. I thought whatever evil Hera had cast upon this place had not infected him yet.

I was wrong. Just as Hera said, I was a fool.

I moved to where he knelt. I tugged at his arm gently at first, then harder. He brushed me aside as if I were a gnat, an irritation. I ran my fingers through his hair. Still, he did not glance away from the surface of the pool.

Panic formed a lump that threatened to choke the breath out of my silent throat. I peered into the pool to see what it was that held him so rapt. It was only his own reflection, I realized, bemused. Yet he gazed at it with a longing that had never been there when he looked at me.

Desperate, I yanked his face towards mine, forcing him to meet my eyes. He cursed and spat. A glob of spittle stuck to my cheek.

"Foul witch," he muttered with such disgust that tears sprang to my eyes.

I threw my head back and howled wordlessly at the sky, at Hera, at Olympus. How dare they take from me the only thing I held dear in my pathetic, endless life?

Narcissus did not speak to me again. He did not even look upon me again. Everyday, I silently raged and did all within my power to return him to his senses, to draw him away from the rapture of his own reflection.

Nothing worked.

His golden beauty slowly withered. I could only watch. I brought him all the delicacies the forest had to offer to tempt him. Still, he stared at his reflection as if it were his one true love.

Autumn came and went, leaves falling dead and brown from the trees to drift listlessly in the pool. Never did they obscure my love's reflection. The enchantment held him fast.

Then came the day I pushed aside the ferns and did not see Narcissus. I had to stop my heart from leaping. By then, he was a husk of what he had once been. Still, l loved him dearly and would have cared for him for eternity if the gods allowed it.

The gods, of course, would allow no such thing.

I cannot say whether Hera knew what trap she was laying when she cursed the pool. Perhaps she wished only to trap me. We Oreads are known for our vanity. This, too, they say, is in our blood. The punishment she meted out was far worse.

I crept into the clearing, knowing what I would find. His body, emaciated, aged a hundred years, floated facedown in the water. Tears slid down my cheeks, mingling with the waters of the cursed pool. When I finally willed myself to do the deed, I pulled his body from the pool and laid him down amongst the reeds. I smoothed his wet hair, now gone white as bone, back from his brow. I closed his cloudy blue eyes, once so clear, and folded his skeletal arms across his cadaverous chest.

I left him lying there.

The long, high, keening cry built up inside until I could contain it no more.

And so, here I remain. Holding vigil over my lost lover's bones. A cry in the night, an echo in the forest, for the rest of my days.

∾

Kate Seger lives in the Hudson Valley and writes dark fantasy and paranormal romance. She has a voracious appetite for books, music, and all things sparkly. Her fiction has appeared in numerous literary magazines and anthologies, most recently the **Cursed Anthology** *by R&R Publishing. Kate is looking forward to the release of her debut novel* **The Wood Witch's Daughter** *in May of 2020 and more of her writing can be found on Patreon. You can find Kate on Instagram* @ultimate_outlaw_books *and Twitter:* @seger_kate

MOVING ON

C. B. LYALL

The steward peered around the divide carrying a champagne bottle. "Would you care for a refresh?"

Lucy looked down at her empty glass, "Thanks."

A child erupted into screams, showing the Singapore-bound 747 passengers his full decibel range. Lucy gripped her glass tighter. Hours ago, she'd left her own two-year-old screaming when he'd realized she would be leaving him behind. Her arm carried bruises where Adam's fingers had clung on.

"You'll have fun with Grandma and Grandad," she'd said, prying his fingers open.

"I want to come," Sam's bottom lip trembled.

"You'll have a great vacation in London."

Mike's phone rang. "The car's outside. Bye, boys." He turned to hug Sam, but the five-year-old glared and backed away. Adam buried his head, so Mike couldn't kiss him. "You guys, be good."

"Mommy," Adam screamed, thrashing around in his grandma's arms. His distressed shouts still haunted her.

She drained her glass and handed it to the steward wandering down the aisle collecting glasses, and all seatbelts were fastened. The plane taxied along the runway as the crew took their seats. With a roar of engines and speed, the 747 lifted into the air.

Mike was adjusting his club world seat when the steward appeared with their drinks. "Here's to another great adventure," he said, raising his glass.

"Adventure?" The trapped word stuck in Lucy's throat.

"I've told everyone this is your idea. I can't believe how quickly you came on board."

"It's been a wild ride these past two weeks," she said. One flippant answer, and the controls on her life were wrestled from her, again.

"You're amazing!" Mike placed his drink next to the untouched nuts, leaned over and pecked her cheek. "What are you going to have?" he said, flicking through the menu.

Her throat constricted reading the choices. "The chicken probably. You?" Her voice quivered and her vision bleared.

"Are you okay?" Mike asked.

"I'm fine, just a little emotional about leaving the boys." Her mind screamed about the injustice of being uprooted and transported halfway across the world from anything and everyone she knew.

The child at the back of the plane hit a new high note in his protest. "I don't envy them," Mike said, gesturing towards the back.

Lucy turned and watched the father walking up and down the aisle trying to settle the child. She couldn't imagine Mike trying to sooth a fractious child; the boys were her responsibility.

The steward appeared to take their meal orders.

"You look beat." Mike touched her cheek with the back of his fingers.

"Two straight nights sleeping on planes. I don't know how you do it."

"What could be better than thirteen hours of eating, drinking, and watching movies you don't really like before trying to find a comfortable position for sleep?" Mike grinned at her.

"Do you want a list?"

"You'll have a relaxing five days without the kids."

"A relocation trip isn't my idea of relaxation," she said.

Mike's brow furrowed as she met his searching look. She couldn't make out if he only saw her superficially. Or did he use the knowledge gained over eight years of marriage to see below the surface?

The steward came back around the divide with their meals. Mike tucked into his steak, while Lucy pushed her chicken around the plate.

"Lucy," Mike said.

"Hmmm."

"This job they're offering me . . ."

She returned the intensity of his gaze. His eyes held a worried look. "What's wrong?"

"This is a fantastic opportunity for someone my age." He took her hand. "But what if I screw up?" He took a deep breath. "I could stay where I am, but this is the fast track."

"This is a great opportunity for you." She could feel Mike's rapid pulse through her fingers. "Whatever the job demands you'll give it everything you have. What more could they ask from you?"

Lucy remembered scenes in the beginning of their last relocation. Mike's flares of temper at home over the new job's frustrations. She'd become a showpiece at corporate functions. The children were lectured and threatened on how to behave until they trembled.

"Singapore's so different from anything I've done before."

"You love the challenge of new businesses." Lucy watched Mike relax into his chair, unaware of the panic bubbling inside her. She clamped down a wave of nausea.

"What about you?" Mike said. The steward cleared their meal trays.

"Me?" Lucy folded the tray back into the armrest. Her heart raced and her mouth dried. He doesn't want to know, she reminded herself. It's a reflex question. "I'll have the challenges of finding schooling, housing, and getting us relocated."

"That's what I love about you. You take everything in your stride. It's amazing!"

"We aim to please," she said, draining her wine glass. The words "amazing" and "coward" fought for pole position in her thoughts.

Mike leaned over and kissed her cheek. "Staying awake tomorrow might be our next challenge. We should sleep." He reclined his chair wrapped in the blanket and put on his eye mask.

Lucy pulled the blanket up under her chin. She struggled to find a comfortable position. The word "coward" ran an honor lap around in her mind. She should have told Mike the truth. His breathing became rhythmic. Everyone seemed asleep except her.

The steward refilled her wine glass, and Lucy stared into the swirling rich, dark liquid before taking a large gulp. She inhaled deeply and extended her hand to Mike but pulled it back. She'd be shattering the illusion of a happy family, but this couldn't go on. She had the boys to consider. Mike rarely spoke to them unless it was to yell. They now jumped at the sound of his voice and ran to their room when they heard his key in the lock.

When Sam was born, Mike had been so proud. One of Lucy's favorite photos was Mike asleep on the sofa with Sam snuggled on his chest. But by the time Adam was born, Mike's career had taken off. They hardly saw him, and when they did, he was stressed out.

She studied his profile and remembered it twisted in anger when she'd suggested he look after the boys one night. "Get a sitter," Mike had said, hanging his jacket in the hall closet.

"We can't afford my class and help. It's a couple of hours on a Tuesday evening." There was a pleading note in her voice. She needed some adult conversation and stimulation.

"So, let me understand. You want me to ignore my work responsibilities and be your babysitter. Didn't you just say we don't have enough money, but you want to jeopardize my career prospects, our future, so you can spend time at some stupid class? Take an online course."

"I'm asking for a few hours in a classroom with other adults."

"I wish I didn't have to work," he said.

She took a deep breath. "Forget it."

"How can I do that? I'll tell you what. I'll stop working and look after the kids. We'll be poor, but you'll be able to have as much free time as you need."

"I'm sorry I brought it up," she'd said.

"This is a partnership, Lucy. You raise the boys. I go to work. That's what we agreed. Remember, it was your decision to give up work."

She'd backed down, as usual. However, relocations always caused stress and raised tempers and drained the life out of her. She gulped more wine and shook Mike. "We need to talk."

"Now?" Mike struggled to remove his eye-mask. "We have meetings all day tomorrow, and this is our only opportunity to sleep."

"I know that." She started to grow smaller inside and picked up her wine.

"How much have you had?" Mike asked.

"Enough to have this conversation," Lucy said, putting down the empty glass. "I know this isn't the best time, but once we land it'll be too late." Her heart was beating so loudly she was sure it would wake the other passengers. "Each relocation changes us. In a lot of ways we grow, but in other ways we lose something." Lucy could feel every fiber in her body stand on edge waiting for Mike's response.

He stared at her for a moment. "You're not making sense."

Lucy could see his temple pulse throbbing. "You and I are growing apart. You have a great career and the respect of all the people you work with. I have none of that. Each time we move, and I make a place for myself, become involved and begin to feel comfortable, we relocate again. We'll be in Singapore for three years and then have to relocate again. It takes about a year for me to fit in and by then we're starting to look at the next move. And there's the boys."

"Let's not forget them." Mike's speech became very pronounced.

"Children are adaptable, but they miss family. And as they get older, it'll become difficult for them to make friends. They can feel the tension between us each time we move. It's very unsettling for them."

The child screamed again, and Lucy glanced back while Mike didn't seem to hear.

"That was quite the speech. And as we're sitting on a plane headed for Singapore, what the hell do you expect me to do?"

Lucy wasn't sure she would ever be able to breathe in a regular pattern again. She seemed only able to take deep breaths and hold them.

"I'm not sure."

"Great," Mike said.

"I suppose I want you to consider this move from my point of view as well yours."

"Have I ever asked you to follow me blindly? You seemed to want this life until now."

"This last move was supposed to be our last. Signing up for this relocation means I'm also signing up for at least one more. I don't want my whole life to be moving from one country to the next." She wrung her hands. "The problem is, I'm watching your career advance and mine decline into oblivion. I'll be around forty when we leave Singapore. That's a long time to be out of the workforce, if I ever want to go back."

Lucy watched Mike struggle for control. He balled his fists, took a deep inhale and then uncurled his fingers one at a time.

"You said you were happy at home with the boys."

"I am at the moment, because it's my choice. Soon I won't have a choice," Lucy said.

"What about us?"

"I love you, but I'm not sure I matter to you as much as your career does."

He reached over and wiped a tear from her cheek.

"Lucy, we're a team. I couldn't manage without you. You're right; I do want this job, but not so much that I'd risk losing everything else."

Silent tears flowed down her cheeks.

"I could stay where I am. Other offers will come along, but they might not be in New York either," he said.

Lucy didn't recognize her voice when she spoke. "This is about more than a move to Singapore. Depending on what we choose now, we'll be closing and locking some doors forever, and I wasn't sure you'd appreciated that."

"But we'll open others together, won't we?" Mike held her hands and his eyes seemed to plead for her acceptance.

"I think so. You seem to have lost respect for my feelings and opinions. This used to be a partnership of equals, is it still?"

"Of course, it is," Mike said, rolling his eyes and letting her hands drop. "Try to get some sleep. We shouldn't waste the rest of the flight talking." He replaced his eye mask and turned his back to her.

Lucy sank back into her chair and wrapped the blanket around her body like the hug she so desperately needed.

∾

C. B. Lyall's debut novel, **The Virus of Beauty**, was released in 2019. She grew up in Stockton-on-Tees, England. Since then, she has lived in India, Belgium, Hong Kong, and the USA. She currently resides in the Hudson Valley, north of New York City, with her husband. She has three adult sons and one grandson. For more details please visit her on Instagram: @Carolynlyall

LAKE LACHRYMOSE
VICTOR FORNA

The day the lake first saw the boy was sunny. It was kind of sunny like it is after the death of a storm, the kind of sunny where things fell in love—the grass swayed, deeply green, and birds' music filled the air. Cabbage white butterflies fluttered close by too, on the edges of the neighboring woods. As pretty as the day and with dark curious eyes, the boy had knelt beside the lake and splashed his face with her waters. He inhaled deeply, smiling. Like diamonds on a mysterious brown hill, droplets dotted his features. And the lake, staring up at the heavens and the kneeling boy, fell in love instantly, inexplicably, with the latter. It didn't make sense—a lake, a boy?

But when has love ever made sense, anyway?

"Must be the gentleness with which he holds my waters, or those mysterious dark eyes..." the lake tried to justify her feelings the next day. It was neither. She couldn't put her finger on the real reason, as it often was with love and these matters of the heart.

Day after day, the boy came to the lake to cool himself; he splashed his face and sipped a handful of the lake's essence. Always, after cooling himself, he would lay on his back, a straw of grass between his lips, slipping in and out of daydreams. "He has such purity," the lake would say, smitten, "even the wood animals fear him not." Then, she would laugh.

The lake wished the boy could know she was in love with him. Yet, she didn't despair at the forlorn fact that he never would. She was content with his presence alone, even if he was oblivious to her love.

As soon as the boy left in the evening, the lake would miss him as though enchanted, looking forward to his return. The boy never disappointed the lake. He always came back to cool himself. And the lake, ever willing, gave a bit of herself to him each time. At night, if anyone were to peer into her depths, beneath the fishes and dark lakey things, they would've glimpsed her many dreams of the boy: blue and beamful they twirled, like fireflies dancing in the dark.

Moons and seasons went by like that, and the pool only grew fonder of the boy. She learnt his name was Ishmael, and he loved to laugh and nod at things in his head. He also loved to sing of angels, death, and stars with men inside of them. His voice was terrible, to speak of, but if the lake could hark one music for all eternity: "Let it be Ishmael's," she said, "and I would hold glad forever."

Then a day came and went, but the boy did not. It was Friday: days never mattered to the lake before, but love had done it. The lake breathed in and out, fighting off her worries. "It's only a day," she said. But the second and the third days passed too. It rained heavily on the fourth day; the lake wept beneath that rain. "Oh, where are you, my dark-eyed boy?" she whimpered. "I miss you, my dark-eyed boy." But only the night and the trees and the shrubs audienced her sorrow.

If a human missed another human, they could call on the telephone or send a letter or visit on Sunday right after church.

What could a lake do but miss?

Well, miss and hope someday, somehow, the boy would come again… but the years went by, the boy never returned.

The lake found herself in that bleak and dark place lost-love took people and things. A despondent landscape of introspective questions and sharp, blood-drawing answers.

Once, during her dismal days, three men came to the lake. They were unlike the children who came to swim or cool off or make out. They held sticks and machetes.

"I think," said the fat-headed of the threesome. "We should cut a road from the village to this place. This lake could solve all our water troubles, don't you think?"

"You're right," said the one with the machete.

"I believe. Still. That cutting down this entire forest and expanding our settlement would do us more good." The one holding the stick spoke. He wore big boots made from cowhide, and he looked funny in them because his legs were thin.

"Come on. That'd be the death of this lake!" countered the fat-headed man, pointing. He went on to explain how settlements destroy nature.

"Your road will destroy it too," argued thin-legs in big boots, softly.

"Whatever we do destroys," said the fat-headed of the threesome.

As strangers spoke of her death, the lake thought only of one person. The boy Ishmael. How she would never see him again, the love of her life. Her tears flooded her banks.

She would do anything to glimpse the boy one last time. Hear him sing. Soothe him with her waters. Watch him daydream and laugh at jokes only he could hear. "Where has he gone? What could he be going through that had made him forget me? Forsake me. My death is here with these three men, and I will never see you again... come back to me, Ishmael." But only the day and the pebbles and the grasses audienced her melancholy.

After long deliberations, the men agreed they'd let the lake live.

But their coming had scared the lake. Realization of the shortness of life dawned, even for a lake... ah, even for forests and mountains these days. "You never know when they will come for you, humans," the lake said. And became more desperate to see the boy. She shivered. She ached. But what could a lake do?

Nothing! Nothing!

And that only doubled the pain...

How I see it, at the end of the universe, there's a cave. And in that cave, there's a bearded man, who's in charge of how things play out. Papa Fate. A stout man, beard like a river of palm-wine, who coughs up when he tries to laugh and... is remarkably wicked. I wish this telling had a romantic end, but when the boy returned to the despondent lake, at last, what ensued was nothing short of sadistic.

Ishmael had grown up. He had muscles and scars and a stubble on his dimpled chin. Mystery and curiosity no longer lurked in his eyes. Only pain and other miserable things the lake could not understand loomed in their place.

She wished she could know and fathom the things the boy had been through. What took away his youth? His purity?

"Oh, what have you seen, my dark-eyed boy? What have you been through, talk to me…"

The boy didn't—couldn't—hear her, for men of these days were deaf to nature's cries and love. He only splashed his face with the water she gave.

The lake trembled at his touch, ecstatic. "Oh, don't leave me again, darling boy." She had missed his gentle hands. Though calloused now, she still loved how they feltl.

As the waters dripped off the boy's sunken face, he didn't smile as he used to before. Neither did he lay on his back with a straw of grass in his mouth. Nor did he daydream. Nor did he sing of uncanny things.

He sat and drew his knees to his chest. He said, to the evening air and the world, "I am tired. I can't take it anymore." Tears dewed his eyes.

"Take what?" asked the lake, concerned. But no conversation had ever been more odd in its one-sidedness.

No answer came from the boy.

If only the lake could hug him and tell him he was going to be okay. "I am here for you." But what could a lake do, other than love in silence, hoping it was enough?

"No one loves me…" the boy continued to himself.

"But I do!"

"My father… my father… mama doesn't care." He shook his head at unspoken stories, unspoken hurt. He took out a rope from his raffia bag. "I am tired."

"I will always be here to refresh you, lighten you again," said the lake.

"Why must I continue this life?"

"Because what is mine, without you here?" The lake recalled the aches of years without the boy. "Many come to my waters, but you alone make me feel like this—please stay…"

The boy didn't hear her. He went on and tied a noose on a lonesome mango tree.

The lake had longed for the boy to return, and now he had, it was to end his life. Her heart sank. "This is not the answer, my dark-eyed boy."

She wanted limbs to save him. But she was only a lake. She could only watch the horror, and oh, what horror's greater than watching the one you love die at their own hand?

The lake could only watch as the boy climbed the twisted branch of the tree. Watch as he set the noose around his neck, as one would a lover's necklace. Watch as he trembled at floods of memories. Watch as he nodded and said, "I'm better off dead. They are all better off without me." Watch as her dark-eyed boy jumped off the lonesome mango tree.

"No! No!" she wailed.

The pain the lake felt at that moment, as the boy struggled to die and all she could do was watch and cry, no quill or pen or keyboard would ever be able to put down.

And if anyone had visited the lake that evening, this is the picture they would've seen: Limp, the boy's body hung from a tree, swaying side to side. In the backdrop was a blood red sunset, and the lake, all lonely and maudlin.

∽

Victor Forna is a young Sierra Leonean writer who resides in his country's capital, Freetown. This is the first of his short stories to be published. He hopes that through his writing he could help put his country on the map in a positive light. Read more of his shorts on Wordpress: @vfornashapes or his poetry on Instagram: @loneobserver_vf

REMINISCENT OF THE PAST
AINI KASSIM

I watched the park from my workspace and opened the window. The cold evening air rushed into my warm room. The slight touch of the frigid air felt refreshing, so I decided to take a break from my hectic work. I brought an umbrella with me as the sky looked like it would rain cats and dogs later.

"Mom! I'm going to take a walk for a while!" I shouted to my mom.

"Make sure to be back before dark," she replied from across the kitchen.

I inhaled the icy evening air, stretched my body, and sauntered towards the park. My work as a designer was quite tiring, so I barely had time for myself. It had been remarkably long since I enjoyed the fresh air and being outside had lightened my head a little. "*The air feels so refreshing,*" I told myself as I let the cool wind caress my cheeks.

When I arrived at the park, I took a seat on a bench under a huge tree. I looked around. There was a family of four playing Frisbee with their dog, teenage boys playing badminton, and a kid who was occupied with her drawing. On the right side of the playground, I spotted a young couple who were talking with each other. As I watched them laughing happily, it reminded me of the time I spent with Mike. Sometimes, I would scare him from behind when he was immersed in his paintings and watched him drop his brush on the floor. He would jokingly scold me and ask me to sit next to him to watch him paint a sky full of brilliant shining stars. Or, this one time where he teased me, saying I was too small, and he could barely spot me whenever I stood in the crowd. "*Don't get angry! You look just like a big teddy bear,*" he joked while pinching my face. I sighed heavily. Those memories felt new and recent in my mind.

I stared at the dark sky as I recalled my memories from ten years ago. It was a dark summer evening. It had been two weeks since he last talked to me. I was quite annoyed and enraged at his silent treatment. And then, one day, he suddenly messaged and called me out. When I saw him waiting for me in front of my house with his cute smile pasted on his face, my anger cooled down. We walked slowly as we watched the kids playing soccer in the middle of the park. The tension around us was getting higher as we circled the small playground. I was getting agitated, so I broke the silence.

"Why did you call me?" I asked as I nervously looked at him. It took courage for me to actually say those words.

He stopped in his tracks and turned to look at me. He smiled bitterly. "I—I wanted to apologize to you," were his first words uttered from his mouth.

I kept my silence as I listened to him. I could hear my own heartbeats as I waited for his next sentence.

"I wanted to tell you, but I couldn't. I didn't have the heart to tell you." He avoided my gaze and looked down at his shoes.

Confusion consumed me. "What are you talking about? Is it because of the silent treatment you gave me?" I asked him. I continued, "Are you cheating on me? You want to dump me right now?" I could not hold back my anger, and it exploded then.

"N—No, it's not like that," he said. His voice was shaky, and he kept his eyes on the dry pavement.

"Then what is it?" I asked. I could hear my voice filled with irritation waiting for his answer.

He looked at me. His pale blue eyes seemed to pierce straight into my eyes as he practiced them on my face.

"I'm going somewhere far. We might not be able to m—meet again," he replied as he burst into a cry.

I could not find my voice as the news shocked me. I stuttered. "Where are you going? Even if the place is far, we can still meet, right? Why are you crying? Don't cry! Tell me," I pleaded with him and cried helplessly as I held his hands tightly.

He stared into my eyes. "It's not about far or near. It—It's, today might be my last day with you." He studied my face and waited for my response.

It took me a moment to understand his words. Hot tears rolled down my wet cheek. My voice choked inside my throat and I could not utter a single word to him. "Since when?" I demanded the truth from him. He gazed at the cloudy sky overhead us and answered solemnly. "Exactly two weeks ago. I wanted to tell you, but I couldn't." Tears rolled down his face.

"If you had told me, then I would not have had any stupid thoughts about you. And we could be spending our time bet—" my voice choked in my throat, and I let out a soft cry.

He watched me in silence as I cried. We stood on the pavement until the light rain shower splattered above us. He pulled me towards him and led me to my house as he held out the umbrella he had brought with him. The sound of the rain splattering on the umbrella calmed me. The rain had stopped when we arrived at my house. Sunshine penetrated the cold evening air. "Thank you for your time, Alice. I'm going to transfer to a better hospital tonight. It's quite far from here." He paused. "I'll ask my mom to send you the address later."

I looked at his pale face shone under the dim sunshine. His blue eyes glinted in the sun. "Until when are you going to stay there?" I asked him slowly.

"We don't know yet. I might have to stay there forever." His eyes were full of sadness. "Okay, it's late. I gotta go." He let go of my hand.

I held back his hands. "Promise me, you'll take care of yourself there." Tears rolled down my cheeks.

From afar, I could hear a car approaching us, and then it came to a halt. He looked at the car and hugged me tightly. I could feel his fear and sorrow flowing into my broken heart. Before letting me go, he whispered something into my ear and kissed my forehead.

I watched him as he walked slowly toward his father's car. Hot tears continuously rolled down my cheeks and soaked my face. The car sped through the street and left me alone standing in the empty parking lot. I watched it disappear into the orange sunset on the horizon. His hoarse voice echoed in my head. I clenched my chest as I cried loudly in front of my house.

I will love you forever.

As the storm rolled from afar, its angry rumbling woke me up from my melancholic memories. I stood up and realized that I was alone in the park. I took slow tiny steps toward my house. The memories of that day were buried deep in my mind. Especially the day I got the call from his mother.

"Hello? Is this Alice? I'm Mike's mother. I'm calling you to tell you that Mike has left us. I've been wanting to send you the address of the hospital, but we were so busy with his sudden outbreak."

After getting the call, I quickly packed my things and went to attend his funeral. I could not move on from that day and slept for a few days afterward. My eyes were swollen from crying too much, I could not focus on my studies and even failed my exams.

Even after a few years, I could not open my heart to another person. It was like my heart was buried the day I went to his funeral. It has been ten years since Michael left me, and I am trying my best to live my life. Even though his memories still lived within me, they were disappearing slowly but surely as time flew.

"Why are your eyes red?" asked mom abruptly when I entered the house. "Were you crying?" she pestered again.

I looked at a photo of Mike and me that was arranged between our other family photos. "Just recalling some bittersweet memories," I said as I smiled at my mom.

∾

Aini Kassim is currently studying material engineering in Japan. Aini received a second-place prize for a poetry competition in highschool. You can find Aini on Instagram @yuucat00 and on Wattpadd @YuuCAT

You're Safe with Me

Katherine Gower

My girlfriend's best friend died. They suspect foul play, so really, she's been murdered, but they just need a less scary way of saying that to the family. That word is kind of awful, though, isn't it? So brutal. Straightforward. Murdered. I guess murder *is* both brutal and straightforward. The way she died definitely was those things. She was strangled. The shows on TV about serial killers always say that strangling means it's personal, a lot of passion involved. The victims almost always know their killer too. I think they're investigating the boyfriend. It's always the boyfriend. How does that saying go again?

Can't live with them, can't live without them.

I didn't know Ellie that well myself. I had, of course, met her and had conversations with her, but I wouldn't call her my friend. We were associated due to our mutual interest: Megan. I told the police that too. They came around to speak to Megan, and she asked me to be present. They asked her routine questions – Did Ellie have any enemies? Was she scared of anyone? How was her relationship with her boyfriend/parents/boss/colleagues? Megan could barely get an answer out; she was crying so much.

They asked Megan to keep an eye out and an ear out. If she hears anything suspicious let them know. Megan stayed in the living room while I walked them to the door, and I asked why they said that.

They said, "We can't really discuss details, but we're exploring all options. This could be the start of something more sinister against young girls. Just… keep an eye on your girlfriend."

Of course, I would. I'd keep her safe. That's my one aim of being Megan's boyfriend — keeping her safe, keeping her with me. No one can take her from me. I've admired Megan from afar for too long to let anything silly come in the middle of us. I know what she wants in a man, and I became it. I am it. I *am* her perfect boyfriend.

It's difficult being the perfect boyfriend, though. Especially when something like this is going on; you don't know where you stand. I want to be there for her, but I don't want to crowd her. But I don't want her to think I'm being aloof so she finds comfort elsewhere. I'm not sure how to play this. She's not using her phone, and when I check on the cameras, she's just always in bed. Before, when I got stuck, she would always tell someone what she wished I would do. Then I wouldn't feel so stuck anymore.

I don't like feeling stuck.

Megan's mother invited me over when she didn't leave her room for a few days. She said she thought I was the only one who could help her come out of this depression. I would do my best, I assured her. Megan was happy to see me.

"I think you're the only person I want to see," she tells me. Of course. I am your perfect boyfriend, and I am here for you. "You never think this kind of thing will happen to someone you know," Megan says. I mean, no, it's definitely not the most common cause of death in the world, but I don't think it's the least common either. Prisons have been filled with quite a few murderers – there's so many documentaries about them now. I think it's smart to be aware that this kind of thing does happen, can happen, and probably will happen to someone you know, love, and care about.

I don't say this to Megan, of course. I pull her close and kiss her head and tell her it's all going to be okay.

"They'll get who did it, and then we can all say goodbye properly," I tell her. The funeral has been delayed due to the ongoing investigation. The body is needed for evidence. I think that makes the moving-on process so much harder. Megan can't even begin to move on with me until she's had the chance to say goodbye. Until she gets the chance, I will continue to be here for her. She's taken Ellie's death very hard, but she's safe with me. I can make it better.

I can. Not Ellie this time.

Ellie and Megan met when they were really young, I don't know exactly how old they were, their ages seemed to change each time I asked. They have "literally" grown up together and "literally" did everything together.

Which is great.

Makes for a really strong foundation of friendship that no one else can crack into.

Megan and Ellie told each other everything, and I mean, *everything*. About school, about home, about family, about boys. Megan told Ellie about her first love; some guy named Matt who I'm pretty sure still worked with Megan.

Matt moved away shortly after I met her, though.

Megan also told Ellie about me. I didn't mind that. I know the way we met was really special for Megan. I tried to do a lot of romantic things for her, so I was always sure Ellie would approve. It was a bit of a surprise when Megan told me Ellie had some reservations about our relationship. Ellie thought I was too intense.

A bit weird.

Creepy.

Megan reassured me she didn't think those things, and if I just met Ellie it'd be fine, she'd love me. So, I did meet Ellie.

But she still didn't like me.

Megan and Ellie argued about our relationship. Ellie based it all on her "instincts," and Megan said she was just jealous.

They didn't speak for a few weeks after that.

Megan was upset at first, but I helped keep her mind off of it. I planned amazing dates and took her away on holiday, and she was happy. I showed her that she had other friends, and she could be friends with my friends. I kept her included – I didn't want her to feel lonely. I showed her that she didn't have to be friends with Ellie. And she really was happy.

Ellie was making her feel bad all the time. She was saying horrible things about me, and Megan didn't like that. Megan even said, "If she doesn't support our relationship, she's not a friend to me," so they weren't friends.

When Ellie wasn't speaking to Megan and wasn't saying horrible things about me, Megan was happy. She was herself again. It was so good to see.

Then Ellie came back. She wanted to apologize, and they were going to meet up for drinks and have a 'girls' night.' Megan was apprehensive. She didn't want to go, but she said she still loved Ellie and wanted to hear her out. Maybe they could be friends again, but only if Ellie promised to leave me alone. I don't think Ellie did that, as Megan came back even more upset.

It really sent me over the edge to see Megan like that. She cried all night in my arms and eventually fell asleep. I knew that in order for Megan to be happy again, Ellie needed to go.

When I went to see Ellie, I swear I only meant to scare her a little.

Tell her to back off.

Our relationship isn't her business. I told her Megan was happier with me and safe with me. Ellie called me crazy. She said she knows I did something to Matt. His roommate described me exactly as the person who saw Matt last in the bar before he 'left.' She said she was going to tell Megan.

She said Megan would leave me.

See me for what I really am.

She kept talking and she made me really angry. So, I pushed her really hard, and she fell onto the floor. I held her on the floor until she stopped talking.

Matt's body was never found, so they can't prove anything even with a description of a man. But I couldn't let him take Megan.

Matt was planned. I was careful.

Ellie was a mistake. I just left her there.

Although I didn't mean to kill her, I did think Megan would be happy knowing she couldn't say any more bad things. Knowing she couldn't hurt us anymore and that we could live happily. I intended to tell Megan what had happened, and she would be so happy with me. Then I saw her crying, and I knew, I caused that pain. I had hurt her. I never intended that. I never wanted to hurt Megan. She keeps saying, "What if I'm next?"

I tell her, "You're safe with me…"

∽

*Katherine Gower is a new aspiring author from the UK, writing variations of short stories and young adult novels. "You're Safe With Me" is her first published piece of work and hopefully not her last. Her twitter is: @kateyg_*

SECTION THREE:

BATTLES OF THE HEART, MIND, AND SOUL

THE UNPAINTED PORTRAIT

M.D. JEROME

"**B**ethany, you'll be paired with… Jacob."

The deep timbre of Mr. Borealis stating who her partner was going to be caused a tingle to work its way up her spine to the center of her heart.

Bethany Hart had had a crush on Jacob Lambden since the beginning of sophomore year, and still after a year she continued to hold a torch for the guy.

He'd started at Notre Dame High School that sophomore year, and the school had buzzed with excitement about the new meat. After a month of Jacob's shadowed personality, the buzz had quickly died. He was a mystery, and his features seemed intent on keeping his secrets. Jacob had long black hair curtaining his dark eyes, which were framed by thick spiky lashes. His mouth was always tight-lipped; not out of animosity, he just hardly spoke. He had long pianist fingers that often gripped a dull pencil and the plain white notebook that he held close to his chest. He was an art major and nothing seemed out of his element from paint to charcoal. He could do it all… and Bethany was halfway in love with him, if not all the way.

She'd never been noticed despite her efforts; now she was granted the opportunity to finally get Jacob Lambden to love her back. *Thank you, crappy Poli-Sci!*

"This is a small project, but it has a tight deadline. So, you'll need to get with your partners ASAP; we start presentations in three days."

The whole class let out a thunderous groan which Mr. Borealis mockingly battled back with his stool, appeasing the class with their laughter.

"I know." He continued. "But senior year will be harder, and presentations are demanded in every class. You will all thank me later, I promise." The bell rang and class was dismissed. The scraping of chairs and textbooks banging filled the room as voices rose in octaves, "Don't forget to meet with your partners!" Mr. Borealis yelled.

* * *

After getting a reluctant Jacob to meet after school, Bethany was antsy to get out of her last period class. Of course, it had to be history. Currently, they were watching a short film on the Cold War. Their teacher was out for the day, and a substitute teacher was covering the class.

"You gotta just take charge. Men like that."

"I don't know, Kelsey…"

"Trust me. I've done it before. I know."

Kelsey was the socialite at Notre Dame, and she surrounded herself with only those who could make her rise in social status. Currently, that was Tiffany, Makayla, and Winnie AKA Winfrey. Sadly, they were all in her last class. She usually drowned out their pitiful and shallow conversations, but today's topic pulled her in.

"But aren't you worried about… rejection?" The high-pitched whine of Winfrey's voice was her signature; it was usually paired with a glossy pout that unfortunately worked on all the boys.

"No, stupid. You taking charge relays confidence. They'll be too busy being in awe of you to second-guess anything. Make your move, *then* ask Matt out." She heard the click of Kelsey's compact mirror snapping shut, which she envisioned as a judge slamming her gavel. Case closed.

Bethany usually didn't concern herself with their warped version of the high school realm; there were more important things happening in the world. But today the subject and specifically the advice crowded her mind. Did guys like it when a girl took charge? Was there less chance of rejection? And, more importantly, did she need to take this risk with Jacob? She carried the questions with her throughout the rest of eighth period. After the bell rang, she waited outside near the football field for Jacob. Her backpack was full, and her head was even fuller.

The grass was prickly under her kilt and littered with dandelions and wishing weeds, as she liked to call them. The sun was out in all its magnitude, not a cloud in sight. The breeze blew through her tangled hair, catching the wishing weed she twirled in her hand, holding the wish of her heart as it flew.

She'd kiss Jacob today, no more waiting. She'd been in love with him for over a year and was old enough to distinguish the difference between love and infatuation.

Spotting Jacob trekking his way toward her in the distance, she noted how his khakis dragged behind his feet. He carried a navy colored sweater, the exact replica of her own. He was only wearing his white polo, now faded to off-white from over washing. It was clear the only thing he had purchased in compliance with the uniform code was the sweater carrying the school's crest; everything else looked to be hand-me-downs. Bethany didn't know much about his home life, besides the fact that it was only him and his dad. From the whispered gossip, his father was a drunkard who worked as a handyman. According to Sara Price, her parents had hired him to renovate their basement over the summer, and he never finished the job. Sara said he just wouldn't show up most days.

Jacob's footsteps were inaudible as he crunched the dandelions under his scuffed boots. Cascading her glance upward, eyes shielded by her hand, their gazes connected, and she felt her heart pang. His eyes were bottomless. That depth sparked with a soul-deep loneliness that could only be cured by human connection. She recognized it, because she was lonely too, floating in a sea of people who didn't understand her. When she had first met him and their eyes had struck, her soul seemed to say, "Ah, this is the one." They were kindred spirits who needed each other, and she was determined to have Jacob see that too.

"Hi. Welcome to my humble abode," she joked.

"Hi," was his only reply, before sitting cautiously beside her.

She spoke and took the lead. It was obvious by the way he continued to doodle in his notebook he wasn't going to. She talked about the project, what she believed they should focus on, their main topics of discussion, and how they should go about presenting. Although he was quiet, Bethany knew Jacob was smart as he chimed in with ideas that would elevate their presentation. Satisfied with the foundation they had laid out, both professional and not— she slapped her textbook closed. The sound made him jump.

"So, tell me what you're working on now?" she asked, stalling because he was beginning to pack up.

She watched the expression in his face shift. The strain in his shoulders slightly thawed as he moved the hair out of his eyes. The sun caught there and shone light into his eyes as he discussed his canvas for the school's mural. She watched his mouth formulate a whisper of a smile, and leaning in, she kissed him, wanting to taste that secret smile.

It lasted five seconds, but for her, time froze. Her senses overamplified everything. She was the one who pulled away, and they both just stared at each other. Fascinated, she watched as he raised his dirty fingers to his lips, causing the sleeves of his shirt to fall and revealed the markings of a circular scar on his forearm.

"What's that?"

"My dad didn't have an ashtray… did it to teach me a lesson about being a man."

Shocked speechless, she reached for him, and he seemed to realize what he had said as terror took over his features. He packed up his stuff in a flurry of movement leaving without a word.

* * *

The next day, Jacob didn't show up at school. As the day went on, her panic grew to unrestrained anger. Her mind was quickly made up; after school she stomped all the way to his house. It wasn't until she made it to his walkway that she felt her nerves of steel wobble. His house looked… pleasant. The grass was slightly overgrown, the flowers were wilting, and the weeds were taking over. Shutters were half painted and the gutters were clogged with fallen leaves. The windows were cracked open so she could hear the blare of the TV. Walking up, she rang the bell… and rang it again when no one answered. She heard the curse before heavy footsteps grasped the door open.

"If you're selling something, I don't want it."

So, this was Jacob's dad. He didn't have the same graceful limbs or the artful eyes as his son. They were the complete opposite. Jacob's father was a big man with beady eyes and a robust belly. He held a beer in his hand, and Bethany noted the time of day and the fact he wasn't at work.

"No, sir. I'm one of your son's friends… I was wondering if he was home by chance?"

"Jacob's friend? Well, well, a little girlfriend. Guess there's nothing wrong with him after all. Ya, come in, he's upstairs or something."

Bethany didn't bother correcting him, too aghast by his actions. What did he mean by that? Slowly she walked up the stairs, softly calling out Jacob's name as she went. The smell of paint fumes assaulted her nose as she approached a door that she assumed was his by the art posters decorating its frame. Knocking twice before slowly opening the door when she didn't get an answer, she saw him… swinging from his ceiling fan… a chair knocked down under him.

Bethany felt a foggy film take over her vision as she stumbled toward him. A wail tore itself from her throat. Her limbs felt restrained by quicksand as she reached for him, the screams still escaping her lips. His father ran up and pushed her fumbling hands out of the way as she tried to get him down. The creaking of the ceiling fan did not cease as his frail body swung back and forth, and then everything went pitch black…

* * *

She watched from the crowded sidewalk as they wheeled Jacob's covered body away. The authorities had already spoken with her, and, having known nothing, she was quietly shooed away. In her hand, she clutched the sketchbook that had been below his feet. She wasn't sure how she had gotten it. Hoping it would somehow give her answers, she opened it. The book was distorted from the countless times Jacob had clutched it tightly in his grip. The pages were rough under her fingertips and ink stained from his heavy hand. Each page was convoluted with images of males together: kissing, hugging, holding hands. Drawings on top of drawings. Horrid and vulgar words attached to each image. The last page was a sketch of her bent forward, lips puckered. Her face could barely be made out; there were a series of "why's" written harshly over her face. The ink was raw and black, and the pages were nearly torn from how vividly he demanded the question.

Jacob was gay. He had been gay.

It was clear by his journal that he didn't know how to come out or was too afraid to. Suppressed in a home and judged by his only caretaker, he had tried to swallow it all down and hide. If only she had known, she would have talked to him, listened, and held his hand as he embarked into a whole new world. Maybe then she wouldn't be standing on a sidewalk weeping for the destruction and waste of a precious young life.

Author's Note:

Teenagers are like flowers, fragile and easily wilted. It is our duty as adults to protect and guide them. I wrote this story as a call to action in order to better understand the mind of a teen and how silent the cry for help can be. So, listen closely, because you may be given the opportunity to save a life.

∾

M.D. Jerome lives with her family in Houston, TX. She graduated with honors and received a BA in English Literature in 2017 from the University of Toronto. An avid reader with dreams of being a writer until 2014, when she woke from a vivid dream and decided to give it a shot. You can find her on Twitter: @mdjerome_ or Instagram: @m.d.jerome

Loss of the Heart
Maximilian Beindorff

In a small tavern not far, only a few blocks from here, chess games are played. The games have taken place there for many, many years. In all of these years, one duel stands out above the rest. To explain this properly, however, I must go back a few months to recount its history.

There was a young man by the name of Dmitri, who was always very bright. However, he used this brightness to blind others rather than to illuminate their paths. As chess is a game played by those of sound mind and strategic forethought, Dmitri seemed a natural. For years, he worked his way through the city, from gaming house to gaming house, beating all those who stood in his way. With each victory, a small puff of air inflated his ego. The last stronghold he had yet to capture was the aforementioned tavern.

Working his way from table to table in a matter of months, he conquered all those who considered themselves—and truly were—the best chess players in town. Dmitri let them know that he had defeated them, lest they forget who the king of the board in chess was.

One night, the old men of the tavern gathered together to discuss the case of young Dmitri and what they were going to do about him.

"How can we let this child ruin us?"

"He is making us look like idiots who have never played this game. He must be made an example of!"

"But how? None of us can actually beat him."

Having seemingly reached the impasse they all already knew of yet had never brought to the light of day, they thought long and hard about any possible solution. Then one of them said, "Do any of you remember that old man who lives on the edge of town? He used to come to this tavern to play us once in a while. No one has ever beaten him either as far as I can remember. Can any of you say that they have?"

"Well…yes I remember that…oh, no, wait, he did defeat me."

All the other men agreed that they had also never tasted the nectar of victory's chalice when facing this man.

"Then I shall go tomorrow and ask him if he would do us the honor of engaging Dmitri in a game of chess," proclaimed the man who had put forth the idea, which was met with great elation and support by the others.

* * *

Very early the next day there was a knock on the old man's door. "Come in, the door is open," a voice from inside informed. The door creaked open, and the idea giver from the previous night entered.

"Dear sir, please accept my humble apologies for disturbing you. My name is Vlad, and I come from the chess tavern you frequent infrequently."

"Ah yes, I have not been there in months. How are the old men there? I guess I should say young since they are all younger than I am," the old man chuckled.

"They have a favor to ask of you, one that they hope you will indulge them in and for which they may be forever grateful to you."

"Well, this has to be a mighty big favor."

"Why do you say that, sir?"

"Because forever is a very long time to be grateful for. Yet still not enough…," the last part of his sentence trailing off into a personal sentence rather than a public one.

"Yes, sir, it is quite a pressing issue, and if you do not mind I would like to take a minute of your time to inform you as to what the circumstances are."

"No need my friend. I already know what you have come to ask, and I shall agree."

Baffled by the response, Vlad asked, "Sir, how could you possibly know what I mean to ask?"

"Your assumption of my ignorance as to the goings-on of this town in which I have lived all my life is the source of yours. I know very well of the young man named Dmitri and his prowess of our beloved game. I shall be there tomorrow. Be safe and may God keep you."

"Thank you, sir. May the same be afforded to you."

* * *

The next day, all the men of the tavern refused to play Dmitri, knowing that the old man would be along presently.

"You cowards!" Dmitri bellowed throughout the tavern. "All of you are afraid of defeat."

"Calm yourself, young Dmitri. I will play you." The old man had appeared in the doorway, observing the spectacle of youthful boasting for a bit.

"You, old man? Can you even move the pieces on the board?"

"There seems to be only one way to answer your question. Shall we?" the old man said motioning to the chess tables. Dmitri, with a great smile upon his face, took his seat.

"Young man, do you mind if I sit there? My faithful companion, time, has robbed me of the full use of my back."

"It does not matter, old man. I could beat you from across the room!"

"That will not be necessary, unless you have not washed yourself today."

The tavern erupted into a great laughter which was quelled by the look Dmitri gave them.

"You will pay for that comment, old man."

"The bill will have to be served soon for the days I am to spend on this earth are no longer in the double digits."

"Stop the talk and let's begin."

"I am waiting for you to start, it is your move," the old man explained, pointing at the chess board.

So the great battle of the small tavern had begun. Move upon arduous move was watched by all. The only man who seemed to have no mind for the game was the old man playing. He talked and laughed with those who sat around him, seeming to take this as an opportunity to catch up with his friends. As a result of this negligence in concentration, he started to lose pieces at an alarming rate. All the men of the tavern started to be concerned and resigned themselves to the fact that Dmitri shall never be defeated. When only six of his pieces were left, the old men looked at the board, then at Dmitri across from him, and began to speak to him these words:

"When we lose at something, does it expose our own mortality? When we weep, is it for the opportunity that is lost or because it might never come again? Has the combative character of man's lower nature taken a hold of our souls, so that we must constantly measure ourselves against others we do not know and even our friends? By believing Darwin's Laws of Nature, we have also assumed that this is true for human nature. But how, with all its multitude of differences from all the creatures of the animal kingdom, do we believe that, in our evolved state of civilization and cohabitation, we must dominate those whom we perceive as weaker? Is it because it is less painful to dominate the other than to open your heart towards the unknown, even when that unknown is the soul of a fellow human being? The word unconditional has assumed a status in our society that makes me wonder when exactly our children shall walk through the museums of tomorrow and, among the Roman spears and Pharaoh's headdress, they shall find this word and ask their parents what it means. Their parents will have to look at them and say that they do not know. That language of the heart died many years ago."

"Check. I guess you are about to find out, judging from how you are playing," boasted the young man, the splendor of the impending victory over his foe already making itself at home in his heart, fluffing the pillows on pride's couch.

"Checkmate. Good game my friend. Same time tomorrow?" the old man smiled at him, rose from the table and walked out of the tavern into the street as the whole tavern stared at the board.

∽

Maximilian Beindorff was born in Germany before living in the US and Canada for the greater part of his youth. There, he was exposed to the great literary tradition of the English language with writers, such as Whitmann, Gibran, Huxley, and many more. His influences also include Rumi, Poe, Tagore, and many religious texts from around the world.

WAR TORN

LUKE ASPELING

Irving Abram

Irving Abram was drawn toward something. A sound pulled him in. The call of voices rose from the Earth and washed over him. With each breath, the wave of indistinct praise receded to its source before covering him once more.

The roaring drone of voices guided him. Rays of sunlight shone through the canopy created overhead; thick branches were interwoven fourteen times over and some even connected from trees that were as far as fifty feet away, bending and twisting new strands with each step. The natural mosaic spread out perfectly across the dew-covered grass. His tentative steps soon turned into authoritative strides. Shrubs and trees peeled back, unveiling a path leading to a hill with a blinding white light behind it. Irving's aged body and taut skin weaved masterfully through the cluster of flora. The light shining toward him created a silhouette, and with every breath, the skin around his ribcage tightened, momentarily clinging closer to the bones it housed.

The intensity of his steps increased every time the soles of his feet nestled into the ground and became so powerful that each movement caused the ground around him to shake. Branches fell, trees toppled over, and incandescent leaves rained down.

The drone of voices now blended into one unified surge of the human spirit, pulsating. "The sound is moving," Irving thought. Like the waves of the ocean drawing back calmly before crashing into the shore, each rise and fall in pitch and tone mirrored his steps, and all he could see in front of him was a beaming light cutting through the trees in the distance.

Irving reached the hilltop and what he saw next brought him to his knees. The light, like burning magnesium, hovered over men, women, and children. There were so many that if he tried to see where the crowd ended, he would surely be looking at the edge of the world. "They travel down broken roads and find their home on the horizon," he said to himself as he recalled a conversation he'd had twenty years ago with the British missionaries travelling the inner Cape Colony along with the Circuit Courts. Irving was the first colored man to work for the Courts, and because of this, he wasn't seen as colored at all. Nor was he regarded as white. None of that seemed to matter as he instinctively began to pray, lifting his hands and offering his broken body as worship to the Lord.

Irving started to feel tears stream down his face. He knew that it was a vision, a fifteen-year prayer answered. He knew that in reality he was still chained to the walls of Section K; a pool of blood forming at his feet, his ribs broken to the point where half of his body was sagging and disfigured, and he could hear the chains slowly approaching his cell. The horizon was replaced with the grey bars of his cell door. Yet, something at the end of the corridor caught his eye.

He saw a table in the distance, pure white. Perfect. Peace spoke to him, and Irving recognized the voice. He inhaled through his shattered ribs and his burning lungs. He breathed fully for the first time in months. He breathed again and the burning subsided. His body was never fully healed, but now there was a table where his enemy used to stand.

Henry Abram

It's 1951, and a clean-shaven, well-dressed young man with a face that boasts an age closer to fiction than fact strutted past the degenerates on the corner of Afi and Huy Streets. He threw a wave over his shoulder before turning onto Huy Street as they called out to him, making reference to the color of his suit, "Ahoy groen-man!" The young man was Henry Abram, and on most nights, he would greet the self-proclaimed degenerates and entertain their jokes. Tonight was different. He didn't want them to see the bruises around his wrists. He didn't want them to know that he had been detained last night. He didn't want them to know about the lashings on his back or the bruised lung. This was a community where words moved quickly, and in an instant you could find yourself exiled in your own home. Henry knew the great lengths the community would go to protect themselves, but something was about to change.

"Tonight, we will be the linstock that fires a new hope directly through the heart of Africa. Tonight, we will be free for the first time." These were the words written by hand on the crumpled pamphlet in his left jacket pocket along with the coordinates for the meeting. Reaching for it one last time, he attempted to recapture the feeling he got when he first read it. His faded brown leather Oxfords began to move with rhythm and quickened still as he took a left onto Rhys Street and then a quick right on Hullet Avenue. The click and clack of his shoes added to the soundscape of distant chatter, house number six always tuning their broken radio at exactly 19:00, children's skipping ropes scraping the tar, leaving enough room for the pitter-patter of feet accompanied by shrill laughter, and a singular dog that would surely drop dead if it didn't alert its owner to every change in the environment. Still staring at the pamphlet, he took another right onto Lot Street.

Henry had always been fascinated with South African streets and how the orange light would cascade over every ripple and bump of the concrete, falling into the potholes engulfing the pavement and a portion of the street in a luminous flame; even the white lines became orange. This made him remember how the children used to scream, "The floor is lava!" before they all ran back home. The first one home got to be the first one to hide, and the last had to seek. The only way to really appreciate Cape Town is to walk the streets, because there is not one street that does not lead to another. We are all connected, and with this thought, the corner of his mouth curled up, forming a subdued smile. He turned left onto Gruis Street.

As Henry walked, he put the pamphlet back in his pocket and looked up only to be shaken to his core. The world around him went completely still. His hands began to shake as adrenaline coursed through his body, and his throat dried up to the point where each hurried breath burned his trachea. For the first time today, he was walking on the right-hand side of the road; he had crossed over without thinking. In his world of *"ja meneer"* (pronounced as yaar muh-neer, on account of Henry's "white way of speaking") and *"nee meneer, skies, jammer,"* in a world where he had been groomed *"tot links"* and *"net blankes"* and in a world where he was too white to be colored and too colored to be white…he froze. Helpless under the burning ember that had caught him red-handed, feeling its heat surge through the crown of his head staring at the policeman walking toward him, he looked down…the floor is lava.

Frederick Abram

The sound of a new tomorrow reverberated through Janesly Auditorium. Every stomp of the foot and clap of the hands seemingly in tune with another, voices were raised so loud that many, if not all, had forgotten that they were oppressed, or maybe they had just stopped caring. The sound was beautifully deafening, as many blended into one as African voices rose, men and women gave way for their spirits to cry *"Nkosi Sikele i'Afrika."* Five hundred students gathered to show solidarity as another member had been claimed as a victim.

One such student was Frederick Abram, a dark-haired, slender colored male. This was his first time at a memorial service for a girl named Claire Tyler, and it resonated closer to him than anyone else because not only had they been dating…but he saw it happen. He tried to fight, but the assailant had smashed in his head, causing him to fall in and out of consciousness as he heard Claire's screams.

Prior to the meeting, his great frustration was with how normal a godless world had become. At this thought, he recalled his grandfather's diary. Irving used to write while travelling, and one piece stood out with Frederick, "Don't they see the result? Everything on Earth will remain on Earth, but we are not of the Earth, so our concern is not below but above." He opened his eyes and saw the unified voice and, astoundingly, hands were raised. The national anthem was sung again and again. Tonight was a call to action for the fulfilment of promises made 25 years ago. Frederick was born free, and he always wondered if that were true, until tonight.

With candles adorning the auditorium and every voice now beginning to crack due to the vociferous nature of their singing, Frederick felt the significance of this one night. He understood that moving on as though nothing ever happened would be a greater crime than the one committed against Claire and the majority of women in South Africa. With the sound in that room, each student was making a promise to one another saying, "Never again will we gather under these circumstances." Bleed and cry, bless the nation. Let us run towards our African sunset and rest on the golden waters of tomorrow. This became the slogan for what came next.

∽

Luke Aspeling was born in Cape Town, South Africa. This is his first work piece of work that has been published. He is influenced by classic storytelling but aims to make stories that are relevant for Africa yet still appeal to the rest of the world.

TILL THE BATTLE'S END
BY KRISTALYN A. VETOVICH

They'd met before, Charlie and the beast. Always the same circumstances, always the same weapons—claws versus blade—always here in this small assemblage of trees, away from anyone Charlie knew. Not once had she bested the beast. Never had she come close.

But her confidence never wavered. They would face each other. Charlie's sword held firm, and the beast, with its sickly sweet smile, welcomed Charlie in the only way he ever had: with claws on display to remind her what was coming.

With a nod from both, as usual, they lunged for each other. The sound of metal scraping against a bony claw was a welcome thrum in Charlie's ears. This was a release. Even when the beast knocked her back into the sturdy trunk of a tree and the sharp thrill of pain ran to the base of her spine, it was better than having to tell others what she was thinking… what she felt. They always asked, but how could words describe it?

The beast never asked questions. He did all the talking—most of it the slinging of insults.

"A bit slow today, Charlie. Trying to stretch our time together?"

Charlie only smiled and hefted the sword to swing at the beast's shoulder. He dodged the blow. He dodged them all. Charlie couldn't recall ever landing a hit on the beast, but he would follow through once the battle bored him. Yet he always returned to her, looking for another fight. That was the nature of their relationship: hatred toward each other but a love of trying to wound.

It had started years ago, when Charlie first came to this small clearing to brood over the problems life seemed eager to deal out. The beast had been there, waiting, with a grim solution on his lips.

"Are you even trying, Charlie? You must defeat me someday, you know. Or I'll grow tired and put an end to you."

Sweat ran a cold line down Charlie's temple. It was never pleasant to remember that there would be an end one day. If someone had to win, it should be her. It was only right. She had to try. The beast had made it clear over these past years how to defeat him. She was aware of his weakness.

With a shout, she heaved the sword into the air and brought it down over the beast's head.

Blocked again with a swipe to her arm as punishment. He left a thin line of red down her forearm, and she lunged again, trying to even the score with a slash to his belly. He leapt back with catlike reflexes and leered.

"Not good enough!" his voice echoed off the trees and back to Charlie's ears. Words she had heard all too often. Words that had brought her to this clearing from the start.

A flare of anger bubbled up through her numbness—enough to drive the sword toward the beast's neck.

The beast deflected with one hand, loosening the sword from Charlie's grip and slinging it across the clearing.

"Have you come here to play, Charlie, or have you come to win?" he reprimanded her. "I'm not even the fiercest monster you could face. Your strength is not becoming that of a true fighter. You disappoint me."

Charlie's eyes pinched into a glare. It was no surprise that the beast was disappointed. She had disappointed many—and accepted it—but it didn't make it any easier to hear.

As she hurried to recover the sword, the beast gripped her wrist in his claws, pressing hard on the cut and making it sting.

"If you claim that sword, it had better be with determination. Make an effort, or, so help me, I will end this today. Show me what you've learned."

When he released Charlie's arm, he left three more scrapes for good measure. The skin flared and reddened around them, but Charlie felt only the thrill and determination of battle. Adrenaline and endorphins had begun to flow. If it was an effort the beast wanted, that was what he would get.

Maybe today would be the day. Maybe today Charlie would exploit the beast's weakness and fell him. The clearing would be calm and quiet, and it would be hers alone.

She made a show of spinning on a heel and striding toward where the sword stuck in the ground. She drew it from the damp earth and brought it down with the graceful skill only practice could give. No more games; it was time to dance.

Charlie was familiar with the weight of the sword, the balance between the blade and the hilt, and accepted it as an extension of the arm that held it. Breathing deeply, she shifted between one foot and the other, readying to move light and quick and float across the clearing if necessary to catch the beast off guard.

"Yes!" the beast drew out in a long, pleased tone. "That's it. That's the child I've been grooming for battle. This is what I want to see. Now, show me what you can do with your skill."

Charlie's eyes opened to reveal flares of challenge and arrogance. The day had come: their finale. The blade was sharp—as sharp as the beast's claws would ever be. Charlie had the advantage, if either of them did. The blade was long; it could put distance between them and strike at the same time. Why had she not thought to use it to its potential before now?

She let instincts take control. One foot moved, and it was all out of her head from there. Arms moved on their own and feet skipped and strode in circles. The blade spun over her head and sliced across the back of the beast's shoulders, eliciting a feral cry that spooked the birds from their perches in the trees above them.

That was it—Charlie's first point in their twisted game. Anything was possible now. Victory never seemed so attainable, but here it was within sight. She brought the hilt of the sword down into the beast's lower back, drawing out another roar, and she spun away, lowering the sword to block its next strike.

The beast, shoulders heaving with rage, bared his sharp teeth and tipped his head to the side. His pupils had gone dark with bloodlust, chasing all light from his eyes. He lowered his shoulder to make his next move, but Charlie knew the beast well enough to anticipate his favored attacks.

That shoulder had knocked Charlie to the ground many times, leaving an opening for the beast to beleaguer her with blows and scratches, and that would be the end of their time together. She never recovered enough to fight once the beast moved the brawl to the grassy forest floor.

But that did not happen. As the beast charged, Charlie stepped aside and brought the heel of the blade down at the back of his neck. With a grunt that sounded something like approval, the beast hit the earth and tumbled to his feet, a hand pressed to his neck where Charlie had struck.

He attacked again. Without thinking, Charlie slapped his clawed hand from the air with the flat of the blade.

The beast curled his fingers into a fist intended for Charlie's gut, but she knocked the side of his head with the sword handle, making him see stars and roar in frustration.

The beast became reckless, unleashing a flurry of uncalculated and hasty attacks that Charlie blocked and countered with ease, until the beast had had enough abuse. He dropped to the ground and swept a leg at Charlie's feet, but even that failed.

Charlie leapt back and out of the beast's range. She tripped to the ground, but rolled to steady feet without hesitation, face set downward and glazed over, ruling every movement with pure instinct rather than reason.

Another swipe, another parry. Another punch, another blunt blow to the softness of the beast's side. Then an elbow to his temple, and finally the tip of Charlie's blade to the beast's jugular.

He did not rise. He looked at Charlie with awe for a moment before his face shifted toward a sneering pride.

"You've had this in you all along?" he inquired, half surprised, half exhilarated. "Why have you kept it from me?"

Charlie's jaw set itself firm. If the beast had seen her skill before now, their time together would have ended and—the realization hit at the same moment the beast struck with the back of his meaty hand—Charlie wasn't ready for this to end. What would be left without these mornings in the glade with the beast proving that life was a loathsome struggle? Victory meant a continued struggle to never lose again. Victory gave too much hope for the future and survival in a world bent on beating Charlie down. Fights with the beast were much more tolerable than facing the entire world with a strength she did not have. Better to tire by the beast's claws than by the judging looks and whispered lies of peers who called themselves friends to her face.

"Well done." There was a resigned tone in his voice that Charlie couldn't bear. "You've bested me. Now finish this, and face what's ahead of you."

He gripped the blade with his own hand and pressed it further against his neck, drawing a bead of blood, but Charlie resisted him.

She would not. Instead, she tugged the blade from the beast's grasp, leaving him hissing as it sliced his palm and fingers. The sword was thrown to the ground, followed soon by its master.

The knees of Charlie's pants soaked through with dew sent a chill that brought her back to the moment, kneeling before the beast under his disgusted gaze.

"Why have you retreated?" the beast demanded, pushing himself to stand tall and overbearing. "Get up."

He took up the sword and rested the blade on Charlie's shoulder—to either knight or to behead.

"You will take this sword." There was no room for questions. "You will stand and face me till the battle's end."

When she didn't move, the beast took it upon himself to yank her up by the collar and shoved the sword against her chest.

Without thinking, her hand drifted to catch the handle as the beast let it go.

"Raise your sword."

She did, but it hung in the air like it was hanging from a string, rather than held aloft by a strong set of hands.

"I could kill you, child. Do you not understand that?" He looked away, hissing air through his teeth. "Perhaps I should have, if this is all the fight you've got."

Charlie stared at the grass, numb to the insults.

The beast sighed and shook his head. "I don't want to kill you, Charlie." They'd both understood this before, but this was the first time either of them had admitted their stalemate out loud. "I see a strength in you that is untapped, and I will draw it out of you if I have to bring you to within an inch of your life. I will show you what you're capable of—and then I will leave you."

Hot tears stung the corners of Charlie's eyes. His leaving was what she was avoiding. Why take on the world when the beast was challenge enough?

"You're meant for more than this. Don't you understand?" The pleading in his voice surprised her, but not enough to change her mind.

What did he expect her to do? Talk to someone? Tell them of the feelings that wouldn't come out in coherent words no matter how hard she tried? These battles were lethal, but they were the only excitement—the only happiness—that Charlie had. Why did the beast want to take that away?

She met the beast's eyes, showing him the stubbornness of her resolve. He set his mouth into a thin line, a soft growl rumbling from his throat.

"So be it."

His hand shot out and gripped Charlie's wounded arm, pressing hard to remind her of the precious pain—the reminder that she was alive. He spun her into his chest, bending her arm in an unnatural way, and whispered into her ear. "If your will is this weak, then perhaps you yourself are a lost cause. My time is wasted on you."

The side of Charlie's mouth tugged into a weird grin, and the beast shoved her away with a repulsed sound behind his teeth. Charlie's cuts reopened, and the high returned.

She turned to face the beast and saw his raised claws looming overhead. Still smiling, her eyes slid closed in acceptance. There might be pain, but between leaving the glen and facing death, Charlie chose whatever the beast offered.

It was a shock when the tearing sensation didn't come. Instead, the beast's gentle hand landed in Charlie's hair.

When she looked, the beast's head was low, his eyes hidden by his messy mane of hair.

"I don't know why I bother," he sighed. "But somehow, I still believe in you, Charlie." He raised his head to meet Charlie's gaze, begging her to hear him. "I know you can defeat me. I am not your friend, and I need you to remember that."

He took her injured arm in gentle hands—somehow more human than ever before—and Charlie's breath caught at the realization that, although their meetings were not over, something had forever changed. Something was lost.

Fear gripped her chest, the heart there beat too fast for her to catch enough air.

"Don't worry," the beast assured her. "I'll see you again, but this cannot last forever." He brushed her cheek with the back of his rough knuckles. "I need you to accept that."

His hand fell, and he stepped away from her. Their time was ending on his call, and despite the sorrow, Charlie still took comfort in knowing the beast's words would bring them back together again.

* * *

She opened her eyes to the white tile of her mother's bathroom, a cat brushing against her legs. The yellow fluorescent light blinded her, and the mirror reflected her tipsy smile.

No one had seen the battle because the beast and his glen weren't real. Not to anyone but Charlie, who stood up next to the edge of the tub, dressed her arm with gauze, tugged her sleeve down to the wrist, and shut her eyes against the oncoming rush of shame at what she'd done. She hid her blade in the usual place, left her shelter to face the terrors of a new day, and vowed never to visit the beast again—knowing it was a lie.

∾

Internationally bestselling author of **Pure Fyre,** *the* **Shifted** *series,* **Driven Fearless: The Complete Roadmap to Facing Your Fears and Driving Forward,** *and more, is an astro-numerologist, speaker, and metaphysical expert who helps people find emotional healing through the joy of High-Vibe entertainment. KristaLyn lives in a treehouse in Pennsylvania with her husband and corgis, Jack and Zelda. Find her on Instagram @TheRealKristaLyn and on Twitter @RealKristaLyn*

BUGGIN'

CLINTON W. WATERS

"**A**m I supposed to be feeling something?" Fletcher looked down at his hand and turned it over. He and Kyran were in Edgefield Forest, near Thorn's End, within the game Selvesquest. Fletcher flexed the fingers in his gauntlet and shrugged, clanking as he did so. "I'm not feeling anything."

"Dude, shut up," Kyran said, his eyes closed, feeling the wind against his scales. "We just have to wait for it to happen. This is where the forum said to go." They stood in silence for a moment. Snow fell from the sky as big, white particle effects. The brown Level 1 wolves of summer had given way to the white, Level 1 wolves of winter that hunted the technically Level 0 white foxes and white rabbits. Fletcher watched as one leapt onto a sheep that had wandered into the forest from a nearby farm. Fletcher bet that if he waited long enough, that same sheep would re-form at the farm and walk its way to this point, just to get mauled by the wolf again. It would keep doing that until the end of time.

He found it hard to listen to the crunch of the wolf's teeth breaking through the sheep's body. "What if I have a bad trip?" Fletcher asked to drown out the squelch of bloody flesh being torn by teeth.

"It's just like anything else. If you think you're gonna have a bad trip, you'll have a bad trip."

"But what if I don't think about having a bad trip, and I have a bad trip anyway?"

Kyran sighed heavily and opened his large, amber eyes; the pupils were tiny slits. It made him look even more annoyed. His tail swished in the snow, leaving long drag marks. "Then you'll have a bad trip. Don't be a pussy," he said, pushing Fletcher. "It won't kill you or anything. No matter what, the game will log you out when it realizes something is wrong. The trick is to—" he stopped, looking at a nearby tree. He grabbed Fletcher's shoulder and pulled him closer. "See that?" He pointed his clawed hand at the trees, and Fletcher could see a fawn fumbling toward them.

"What? The deer?" Fletcher asked, and Kyran shushed him. He pointed to a tree a few yards away, where a wolf was walking its normal route. It seemed to notice the fawn, and in an instant, it darted through the snow. Fletcher wasn't entirely sure what he saw next. The wolf opened its fanged jaws and lunged at the fawn, but the fawn didn't move. The wolf just passed through the tiny deer, as if it were a ghost.

The fawn made a buzzing sound as it flickered on and off, jumping to a spot a few feet away and then snapping back in an instant. The wolf lay dead on its side. The fawn leaned down and began to eat its flesh. A gush of blood spurted up onto its snout. "I—I don't," Fletcher began, but Kyran was pulling him towards the deer.

As they got closer, the trees began to flicker as well. The snow became crystals, falling upward. The sun turned black in the purple sky. The soundtrack of woodland sounds became blips, and the flatline EKG drones were the loudest death could be. Fletcher was aware that his fingers were laced with Kyran's, but Kyran was miles ahead. He was behind.

They reached the deer, and it turned to look at them with blood painting its soft muzzle and splattered on its wobbly legs. Kyran let out a whooping shout. Fletcher had heard it before during summer. Back when they took off their armor and jumped into the lake from the cliffs above, when Fletcher was Finn and Kyran was Kyle, and when they drove Kyle's pickup to the river and made sure no one else was around. That was when Kyle didn't have to tell him to not be afraid. When he was brave and took the leap he had wanted to take for so long. When they jumped together into the fast, dark water. Fletcher felt his head bashing against the rocks below, becoming paralyzed, not able to fight the water flooding into his lungs.

He retched, and pebbles came tumbling from his lips and piled up at his feet. Kyran's snake mouth was unhinged, gaping and wet; he was laughing and laughing. Fletcher was the wolf being tugged from the inside out by the fawn. He couldn't scream. He could only look up at the white sky until he was drifting upwards like the snow.

When he looked down, he saw his cramped bedroom; the walls were closing in on the him that was Finn who lay in the bed on his side. He was crying, holding his phone so that his pale face floated in the darkness. Fletcher didn't have to look at the screen. He could remember the words exactly as they were written. The words poured out of the screen and onto his face, torrents of jet black ink that Finn blinked away numbly. Words that piled on top of each other, slid down his throat, and settled in his belly.

Fletcher couldn't watch himself drown in the words again. But it was too late. They had already congealed around his feet, curling around his ankles. He called out, and Finn turned to him. His eyes were blank as he smiled. Finn shouted out in fear, but he was back in the woods alone with the fawn. It continued to gnaw on the wolf's bones, crunching into them greedily. "Having fun?" it asked him.

"Not especially, no," he replied and sat in the snow.

"That's too bad," the fawn said; its voice soft and child-like. It lapped at the marrow inside the bones. "You don't have to stay, you know," it said to him.

"Sure I do. I can't figure out how to log out." He was scrolling through menus written in his mother's handwriting. They said things like, "I'm proud of you," and, "I know it's tough."

"You know that's not what I mean," the fawn said as it folded its legs and lay beside him. It rested its head on his knee and sighed contentedly.

"Yeah, I know," he said and drug his hand along the fawn's fur. "It just feels like I need to."

"You're not doing anyone any favors," it said to him quietly, sliding into sleep.

"Yeah. I know...."

"What do you know?" Kyran asked, standing over him. "That you just had the time of your life, and I was right all along?" Fletcher looked around to see that the forest was no longer shifting and that the snow was falling as it was intended.

"I'm gonna go," Fletcher said, standing.

"Man. I told you if you thought you were going to have a bad trip, you'd have a bad trip. I was out there swimming with big-tittied mermaids in the stars and stuff. I've never had a bad time buggin'."

"I guess that's where we're different," Fletcher said, looking through his menu, which was now back to normal.

"Hey, don't be mad," Kyran said, stepping close. "I thought we'd have a good time. I didn't mean to upset you. Did you see...did you see your mom?" Finally, Fletcher could hear Kyle's voice, and it felt like a punch to his gut.

"Among other things," he said and looked through Kyran's snake eyes, trying to find Kyle on the other side.

"Oh," Kyran said and stepped away reflexively. "Look, Finn...."

"It's fine," Fletcher said. "I'll see you around, okay?" He found the log out command on the menu. He watched Kyran until he couldn't anymore. He hated the look of troubled silence on his face, of words unsaid pushing out against his lips. When his eyes cleared, he was staring at his ceiling again with tears streaking each cheek. He leaned up in his chair and surveyed the darkness. Would he just wander into the forest again?

∾

Born and raised in Bowling Green, KY, Clinton W. Waters holds a degree in Creative Writing from W.K.U. Their published works include the titles **Futures Gleaming Darkly, Dreams Fading Brightly,** *and* **Vivisection & Other Poems.** *Their work has been featured in university publications from W.K.U. and the University of Regensburg. They are the lead writer for Ionic Comics and their webcomic Variants. You can find Clinton W. Waters on Instagram @cwwwriting*

Section Four:

Searching for Something

The White Wolf Dreams

Jonathan Koven

Clouds vacuumed in quiet, shaving the plateau bone white. The skyline still held a maroon glint, dawn. Surrounded by the glacial mountains, the color was soft enough to miss. Yet, it leaked, coring in the frost a ring of the Sun—where the White Wolf slept.

The White Wolf did dream, as animals do, of her children. When she awoke, their absence bore deeper. Paws tucked under her, she whimpered, though she was glad for the warm light.

A moan replied beyond the massive ice wall. She lifted like a breeze in its direction. *Was it them? Could it be them?* The horizon's sliver opened its gash, pouring not sunlight but a reel of smolder, a singed, boiling haze. From its stain, wind rollicked the lowland, and the White Wolf's spine straightened. She felt summoned.

She limped to the plateau's end at the foot of the hill and pawed at its icy path. She would not be able to climb without slipping. Cold snow huddled, and she cried again. The moan answered, voice cracking like slowly melting ice. There was no way around. To discover the source of this sound, she must scale the mountain and see beyond the glacier's edge.

Hungry, she persisted. It had been days since the last meal. Since the blood-lights first blazed the dead sky above, no pulse stirred on the plateau. Only the White Wolf and the wilted earth had watched the Sun pass overhead. She remembered the nights of tectonic roaring, her paws sliding, slipping, leaping; her stomach grumbling passing the firepits, rich with the nutty fragrance of roasting meat; and swimming—swimming in the cold sea, under the hot smoke—swimming under tides thrashing, between floating glass. She remembered escaping the clip and the shot, the blinding lights, the bone-crackle and splash. She remembered her children but forgot exactly where and when they separated. The details grew more obscured as her hunger grew.

When the White Wolf had escaped the fires and fighting, when she had finally reached the plateau, the roaring had finally settled. Yet, she had not expected the quiet to be worse. Exhausted from the silence, like it was an unending ringing in her ears, she needed sound: a burning desperate plea, a hark in the eve of black night—something, anything—to resound in that emptiness. Then, there had been a moan, perhaps a whimper or a cry. She could not waste this chance.

She howled. A howl came back.

Clawing up the icy hill, she saw a snowbank up ahead. The White Wolf rammed her body against the ice, the cold stinging her snout. Snow scattered, flourishing the air. She rejoiced, carefully climbing where the snow fell, certain not to slip on the wet slide beneath.

Hours later, she reached the summit's crest. She panted heavily, swallowing her own saliva for thirst.

The lights above danced like the swirling blood of civilization. They breathed, threading themselves between stars and milking off into the grey mist. She felt her heels lift her into the flare, where no darkness—no shadow passed at all—the sky a pool, a spinning phosphorescent void, draining sound. Weak, she barked softly. Nothing spoke back.

The White Wolf carefully slid down then chased to the hill's foot on the other side of the mountain. It looked the same, matted with snow and stretching for miles.

There! A silhouetted figure elevating from the blankness. It also lifted, pulled into the hands of spilling colors.

The White Wolf rushed, barking. The reply, louder now, pierced her ears like a siren. She barked again. Something called back. *Was it them? Could it be them?* Like the whorl above, a storm teemed her skull; a sparkle behind her eyes flowered in darkness; a white firework spattered. She could not see anything; only the whiteness of snow and noise itself coursing past her.

She arrived at the figure's edge.

An abandoned boat, sail tattered upon the deck, was frozen in the snow. Splinters of wood littered the ground surrounding it. Her long nails scratched the cold deck, feeling the hollowness inside-and-out. The White Wolf whimpered. The boat whimpered back slower. She had only heard her echo. There was nobody and nothing on this frozen boat, merely the memory of a certain motivation—to go somewhere, to arrive elsewhere. Without a creak, it voicelessly prayed its voyage on the deadest ocean, rocking a hull against imagined waves. Pinned down, it only existed as a silhouette, to be appreciated from afar, to hear the echo of one's last chant, to be realized as distilled adventure—bearing nothing but empty promise.

Yet her echoes, when the White Wolf heard them, boomed the glorious pain of surviving. It proved something, despite her being the only one who listened.

She lay on the tattered sail, cradling her own body in the warmth of dreams. The sky's dancing sleeves continued burning, and the silence resumed.

∾

Jonathan Koven grew up on Long Island, NY. He currently lives in Philadelphia with his fiancée Delana and their cats Peanut Butter and Keebler. His other short fiction and poetry can be found in **The Lindenwood Review**, *Pub House Books'* **Gravitas**, *and Paragon Press'* **Echo**. *His debut fiction novel,* **Below Torrential Hill**, *has been excerpted in* **American Literary** *and* **Toho Journal**. *He is currently querying* **Below Torrential Hill** *for agent representation. You can follow his poetry blog at* onebirdspeaks.wordpress.com.

HIS NAME WAS CHARLIE
KYRA FORGETTE

"**M**om, you didn't have to bring me home. I'm fine," I tell my mother.

"Imogen Crane. You died for three seconds. You're coming home for a little while. The end," she tells me. I sigh in frustration. The car accident wasn't even my fault. It was my now ex-boyfriend, Jake's. He was an idiot.

"Okay mom," I say with a sigh. Defeated.

"I'm going to go get us some lunch. Stay here," she tells me, walking out of the door to go get us Chinese food. I'm surprised she left me alone. She's been a helicopter mom 24/7 since the accident a month ago. I know it's only because she was scared, but I was really getting used to the independence that college had brought me.

"Imogen Crane," a strange male voice says from behind me. I spin around, and look at him wide-eyed. "I've heard a lot about you." He has a smirk on his face.

"Who the hell are you!" I exclaim, grabbing a lamp off the table and raising it towards him

threateningly. He just laughs.

"That's not gonna work, honey. I'm already dead," he tells me. I throw the lamp at him, and he

dodges it.

"Get away from me!" I yell. He holds his hands up in defense.

"Woah, okay. I know how this looks, but I'm being honest. Look me up. Charlie Flannigan," he tells me. "I think you know my nephew."

"Excuse me!" I yell. I want him out, pronto. "I'm calling the police," I say, and pick up the phone.

"Do you really want to be the girl who cried ghost?" he asks me. I put the phone down, and let out a frustrated sigh.

"You have five minutes," I say.

"My name is Charlie Flannigan, and you're the first person who's been able to see me in like

twenty years. With that being said, I don't know why you can see me, but maybe it's because you died for a little while about a month ago. Anyway, I need your help," he says.

"It's a little creepy that you know all this stuff about me, and all I know about you is your name," I fire back.

"Really? That's all you got from that," Charlie deadpans. "Type in my name on your smartphone thing. You'll find out more about me."

"You said I know your nephew," I remind him, as I type his name into Safari.

"Campbell Carswell," he tells me. Cam was also in the car with us the night of the accident, and we've been best friends since middle school. I look up at Charlie, and suddenly I do recognize him. I've seen him in pictures at Cam's house. Cam told me this story once. His mom's brother died when they were in high school.

"You're Miss Charlotte's brother," I say.

"Yeah, that's me," he says. I look down at my phone and see an article from 1993. I click on it, and a picture of Charlie is the first thing that pops up. I skim through the article quickly and look back up at Charlie.

"You were accidentally shot by your best friends, Tommy and Kenny," I say. Charlie scoffs, and his hands are balled into fists at his sides.

"It wasn't an accident, Imo," he growls.

"First of all, don't call me Imo. Secondly, what do you mean? Every article, Cam and his mom,

literally everything says accidental," I reason.

"It's not true. That's just what Tommy and Kenny told the cops. Kenny found out me and his girlfriend at the time, Maisie, were in love. He shot me, and Tommy covered for him," Charlie explains.

106

"So, let me get this straight, you and this Kenny guy's girlfriend fell in love. Kenny found out, shot you, and your mutual friend, Tommy, covered for him?" I ask.

"Precisely," he says.

"No, I"m not helping you," I state.

"Please! I need your help to move on, so I'm not stuck in this purgatory bullshit. And to do that, there's two things. One, I want everyone to know my death wasn't an accident. Secondly, I really just want my diploma," he tells me.

"Okay the diploma thing, is probable. They have it put away at Cam's house, but the proving your death was actually a murder, that's where I'm stumped," I respond.

"Tommy is being held at Southern Hill Prison, on unrelated charges of course, but I think maybe you could go and talk to him. Get him to confess," Charlie says.

"You want me to go to a prison, and talk to someone I know nothing about?" I ask, flabbergasted by the request.

"Cam knows him. Take him with you," he reasons. I laugh.

"Yeah, let me just go tell Cam his dead uncle is sending us to go talk to a known criminal. That'll go over real well," I say sarcastically. Charlie rolls his eyes.

"Please Imogen. I don't have much time left here," he says. "When spirits can't move on, they

become evil. I don't want to be evil, Imogen."

I sigh. I can't believe I'm about to agree to this. I think I'm losing it. "I don"t know," I say, unsure of what to do.

"I only have forty-eight hours. Please," he begs.

"What!" I exclaim. "Maybe you should have led with that bit of information," I snap.

"There's not much time here, Imogen," he fires back. I groan, and call Cam. Charlie gives me a smile. I can't believe I'm agreeing to this. Cam answers after the second ring.

"Hey Genny. What's up?" He asks.

"This is going to sound insane, but you need to get to my house ASAP. I'll tell you why when you get here," I tell him. "Oh and bring your Uncle Charlie's high school diploma."

"Uh okay. I'm on the way," he says and hangs up.

* * *

Cam walks in with the diploma in hand. "Wanna tell me what's going on?" he asks.

"No time," I say, grabbing his free hand and pulling him behind me.

"Genny!" he exclaims once we're in the car. "What's going on?" Despite him not knowing, he starts the car anyway and follows the directions that I typed into his GPS.

"We're going to Southern Hill Prison. We need to talk to Thomas Watson. It's about your Uncle Charlie," I tell him. "His death wasn't an accident. And, you're going to think I'm crazy, but he kinda haunts my house."

"I thought you were crazy before this whole Sixth Sense, I see dead people stuff. Also, what?" he says.

"I always hated that our house was built right next to the school, but it turns out the original building was the old gym," I tell him.

"The one my uncle died behind, I know," he tells me.

"We need a confession, Cam. For Charlie," I say. He nods his head, and the rest of the car ride is silent.

* * *

We arrive at Southern Hill, and security leads us to the room where we'll be meeting Tommy. I'm shaking with nerves. The fact that this is even happening, still hasn't sunk in yet. Cam must think I'm a crazy person? Am I, though? Tommy is led over to the table, and he sits down. He looks between us with a questioning look.

"Who the hell are you two?" he asks.

"I'm Imogen Crane, and this is Campbell Carswell. You knew his uncle, Charles Flannigan," I state. A look of deep despair and regret flashes across Tommy's face. He was probably handsome once, but the long hard years of the life he's been living have obviously caught up to him.

"Charlie Flannigan. I haven't heard that name in twenty something odd years," he says. "I can only wonder why you're here," he adds sadly.

"Was my uncle's death an accident?" Cam asks him. Tommy lets out a long sigh, and I can see the tears forming in his eyes.

"Everybody loved Charlie," Tommy spits.

"Please, Mr. Watson. We need to know," I say.

"Why should I tell you?" he snaps.

"I don't know, maybe to be a nice person," Cam fires back. Tommy narrows his eyes at Cam, and I clear my throat to break the tension.

"I'm sure you could work out a deal to get your sentence reduced, if you tell us," I reason.

Tommy's eyes sparkle, and he gives me a small smirk. It fades quickly.

"All right," he begins. "Charlie and Maisie fell in love because me and Kenny were too wrapped up with getting revenge for always being bullied. Kenny hated that fact, and he had finally had enough. He said he just wanted to scare him. I didn't know he was gonna kill him, honest, but he did." He lets out a long sigh.

"Thank you," I tell him.

"Can we get that in writing, please?" Cam asks.

"Of course, kid," Tommy says with a wry chuckle, and the guards take him away.

* * *

The next morning, the news breaks about Charlie's murder. The whole town was shocked to learn that Kenneth Palmer, a well respected high school football coach and teacher, murdered his best friend decades ago at the same high school he now teaches at. His wife, Maisie, also filed for divorce.

109

I sat down on the bench that my mother installed in our backyard garden. Charlie's diploma, and today's newspaper rest in my lap.

"Well, Imo, you did it," Charlie says, appearing beside me. I jump, but I laugh.

"You gotta stop doing that Ghost Boy," I tell him.

"Well, thanks to you and my nephew, I will be," he tells me.

"Are you scared?" I ask. Charlie shakes his head.

"Nah, I'm relieved. I've been stuck here, watching other people get to live their lives, while I'm trapped as an eighteen-year-old. I never got to marry the woman I love, or have children, or score my dream job. Watching everyone else move on kinda just reminds me I don't get to. So, I welcome whatever awaits me when I finally leave this purgatory," he explains. I nod my head and smile at him.

"Is it weird that I'll kind of miss you?" I ask. I haven't known him long, but I feel like Charlie

would have been a real good guy to know. He shakes his head.

"I'll miss you too, Imo. You remind me a lot of Maisie, and it was nice to finally be able to talk to someone," he says. I set the diploma and newspaper in his lap, and he looks at both with a smile.

"We did it, Charlie," I say with a smile.

"This means more to me, than you'll ever know," he tells me with a smile, and tears in his eyes. He looks like a guy who just had all of his dreams come true.

"Goodbye, Charlie," I say. He smiles.

"Goodbye, Imo," he says. And as quickly as he appeared in my life, he disappears.

"Hey, Genny," I hear Cam say from behind me. I stand up from the bench and turn to face him.

"Hey," I say.

"My mom is elated. She said she always knew. She wanted to tell you thank you, and you should come to dinner tonight," he tells me, walking towards me.

"You must think I'm insane," I tell him. He laughs.

"Let me tell you a secret," he says. "I never once doubted you. We never called him Charlie," he says. I laugh.

"You knew this whole time I wasn't crazy?" I ask.

"Yep," he says. He puts his hand on the side of my face, leans down, and kisses me.

"The only crazy thing here, Imogen, is how long it took me to do that," he tells me with a smile. I smile back at him.

"Thank you, Charlie," I whisper, making both of us laugh.

His name was Charlie. And, I owe my new life, after death, all to him. So, wherever he is, I hope he's happy. Because I sure am.

∽

Kyra Forgette is a first-time published author, but writing has always been her passion. She currently resides in Daytona Beach, Florida, with her boyfriend, Adam. If you'd like to see more of her work go to wattpad.com and follow evantate. You can also follow her on Twitter @kyra_forgette and Instagram @kyra.emily

AN UNLIKELY FRIENDSHIP

BY SIAN FULLERTON

F rank Ebert tripped over the truth by accident. In fact, he'd experienced many misadventures in his life. He was a 53-year-old half-Irish, physically impaired former boxer with a weakness for beer and crack (though his damaged liver and chemical imbalance could handle neither). Frank and Lily blustered through the city like they ran it. Lily was rarely on a lead, despite the omnipresence of by-law officers, cops, and do-gooders. Because Lily was an angel. A black angel with a wet nose and some sort of digestive malfunction that rendered her breath horrendous, she was a beloved four-legged icon of downtown.

Lily had saved Frank, pulling him out of a low point that was dark enough to extinguish the smallest of life-lights necessary to keep a man from sinking completely. So, a bond was forged. Frank never considered himself a family man—Lily made him one. They befriended the dog park regulars and were impressively knowledgeable about the drop-ins. Frank needed to know them all. Each new and familiar face was embroidered into the fabric of that pocket of the city.

Lily's companionship had revealed to Frank that he was capable of love. It was a subject Frank never consciously broached. He ambled through life barely dipping beneath the surface, rarely making any sort of emotional connection with another being. It was just his way. Not a deficiency of character or a roadblock, it was merely a fact to be circumnavigated.

Theirs was an unimpressive house on the east side. Frank and Lily shared a bedroom with each other and two pokey bathrooms, a kitchen and lounge room with seven drifters. Usually it was seven. For a month last year, they were just six, after Penny left. Then Rich had taken over her room, and occupancy occasionally topped a dozen.

Frank never had much money, but his clothes and person were generally clean. He was proud of that. Sober, Frank was very conscious of how he appeared. His mother had taught him little in the way of practical life skills though she had certainly passed on the importance of a manicured façade. So Frank did what he could with what was available to him and relegated his dead mother's thinly veiled criticisms to a locked box in the back of his mind.

His mother had him taking tap lessons at age two, and Frank kept it up until his major rebellion at eleven. He chose a hobby as far from dancing as he could get—boxing. It became a passion, and Frank's love for pugilism never waned even after that final concussion that pushed him out of the ring and into the shiny matching tracksuit of a coach. He still hung out at the Hastings Street gym, though he spent more time socializing than imparting his wisdom on scrappy up-and-comers.

* * *

The falling rain was soft yet persistent against the window. It didn't deter Lily. She whined at the front door until Frank picked up the lead and put his jacket on. They walked down the front steps and headed for the off-leash park on Seymour.

Ray, the owner of a secondhand bookstore on their route, was out front having a smoke. He nodded a good morning and then went round the back of the shop to unlock the door for his assistant. Frank stopped for a cup of tea at the café on the corner, then he and Lily crossed to the park. Most days it was packed with mutts in an excited frenzy, running after tennis balls and peeing on everything. Today was different. The only two beings there were a young boy and an ancient Dachshund.

The boy ran over to Lily as soon as she was through the gates. He asked Ray if he could pet her. "Of course," Ray said. "She's very friendly. Her name's Lily, and I'm Ray."

"I'm Evan," the boy replied. He started throwing a ball for Lily, and the two played together for ten minutes. The Dachshund wasn't troubled that his human was entertaining another dog. She was too busy sniffing and rolling in dead things.

"You've got a good arm," Frank told Evan. "Do you play baseball?"

"No," the boy replied. "Mum can't take me to training. She's too busy."

"You seem pretty strong, for a kid. You can't be more than seven. Here, punch my hands."

Frank held up his palms in front of Evan's face. He clobbered the old man with little precision and surprising force. It stirred memories for Frank. He thought about the last time he'd boxed in a ring. It must be 20 years ago now. His dad was there, drunk but standing, and yelling foul abuse at the other corner. Since then, Frank had helped out a couple of young guys, giving advice from the other side of the ropes, but no one took him too seriously.

"Hey Evan, you ever seen a boxing match? I'll take you to my gym, if it's ok with your mum. She can come too. There's an amateur fight on the weekend." Frank considered what he'd just said and realized how creepy it sounded.

Evan lit up. "That would be awesome," he said. "Mum will be working, so she won't mind. Maybe you could come to my place, and we'll walk together, if it's not too far away. That's our place over the road. Apartment 201 on the second floor." The boy pointed to a small, neglected building that looked 100 years old. It was actually the most interesting edifice around. The neighboring newer constructions were all grey and glass and sharp angles. Evan's building looked worn but vibrant; the rust and plum paint flaking but cheerful.

Frank wondered what he'd just done. A single, older man hanging out with a small boy looked incredibly suspicious. This was stupid, too impulsive. Was he really capable of being with a kid, never having made one of his own? But Evan was so happy. "Ok. See you at 11:00, Saturday morning," he said.

"Awesome. Bye, Lily!" Evan scooped up his smelly dog and bounced out of the park, dodging an overloaded bike taxi to get across the road. His mum would kill him if she found out his plans. It's all right, Evan told himself, I'll keep the cover-up simple and she'll never know. This would be the best weekend since Teddy died.

∾

Sian Fullerton is a published journalist and creative fiction writer, who is inspired by the people and places she encounters on her travels. Having compiled lists of character names since primary school, Sian specializes in emotive short stories with a touch of whimsy.

BASEMENT CURIOSITIES
DANIELLE PAUL

I tend to keep a variety of excuses in my mind, loaded like a revolver, just in case. Although, perhaps I could be truthful for once and admit the droning voices and subtle hostility of dinner parties made me feel hollow; a semi-decent pulse at this party would be delightful.

Hoping to sneak out unnoticed, I slunk from the dessert table to the front door and began to slip on my boots. Suddenly, I felt a presence gnawing at my peripheral vision. There was an eeriness in the entranceway I hadn't noticed upon my arrival—the overwhelming shadow of a rickety, open staircase leading down into the depths of blackness.

What lurked before me could only be an entry to a basement. It looked like a forgotten portal to a mysterious underworld. Most of the faded paint had peeled away from the surrounding walls, what little color remained was a cold, uninviting steel blue. The neglected walls and staircase looked extremely out of place. The rest of the house was painted a vivacious burnt orange with warm abstract figures happily dancing on the walls, protected by shining (and expensive) gold frames.

Behind me, the pretentious dinner guests and obnoxious kitchen noises were becoming more overbearing by the second. Though I was aware of the social and moral faux pas of snooping, my itchy anxiousness longed for soothing silence. An escape into much needed silence would allow me to recover from the excruciating whine of anxiety that steamed from within my nervous bones. The unconcealed gloom of the cellar called my name, cathartic yet brilliantly isolating. Just like my social anxiety.

Only a few feet away, I continued to examine the stairs from the safety of the front entrance. The stairway leading into this black hole of a basement had no handrails. How inviting. A broken ankle would be a mediocre souvenir. But it was too late. The cosmic shadow had already pierced its claws deep into my curiosity and lured me toward its tempting murkiness. And so, I descended.

As I crept below ground level, the temperature plummeted, shocking my bones and pulling a sharp, frosty gasp from my lips. The crude, barely finished staircase was crowded with various sizes of cardboard boxes, decaying from the putrid effects of mildew. It seemed as if the rot from the moldy cardboard had seeped into the grain of the wooden planks. Each time I carefully tiptoed over a sagging box or missing board, the next would groan in anguish under the weight of my cursed nosiness.

Eventually, I conquered the stairway minefield and found myself standing on a disintegrating concrete floor in a room without a hint of warmth. Debris was shoved into every corner of the room, which seemed to stretch on forever. Thick, drooping cobwebs, exposed pipes, and wooden beams jutted from the low ceiling. Unmarked containers, metal cages, and stuffed garbage bags were piled higher than the walls of a cavernous canyon, guarding dark secrets and abandoned memories. The shadows cast by discarded furniture and hot water heaters scurried into the darkness as I carefully edged further into the dungeon-like basement.

A grim reminder of what little life was left in this room, a sliver of weak moonlight barely shone through a single pane window. The meek ray of light was cut short by crumbling mountains of abandoned junk. I couldn't help but taste the chalky grime that poured from thunderclouds of dust. Piles of discarded junk loomed over me like a million bony reapers, each of them grabbing at my living flesh, attempting to condemn me to their bleak, lonely underworld.

With every nervous step I took, the hostility of the room spiraled—repulsing my senses until they were nearly comatose. Lifeless mounds of clothing dangled from the rusting pipes above me, like rows of bloated corpses suspended from the bare branches of a mourning oak tree. Perhaps these clothes once belonged to a loved one, now forgotten and abandoned.

I was so transfixed on the decaying rubble that I forgot what my original mission was – to escape. Suddenly, my thoughts were interrupted by a dry, withered voice creeping out from the darkness of the furthest corner. It could scarcely be heard over the empty, echoing silence looming before me. A painful rash of razor-sharp goosebumps shot up my arms, and a scraping shiver raked down my spine. The faint voice moaned the most damned and haunting words I have ever heard:

"Please... Please help me, I'm chained to the floor. Quick, before he comes back..."

⌘

Danielle Paul is an author currently living in Calgary, Alberta. She believes meaningful art comes from exploring our memories and emotions, which allow us to unearth who we are as individuals. Her other work includes: **An Icy Path to Mortality**, *which is featured in SOOP's memoir anthology* **Women Write Now: Women in Trauma**, *and* **February Warmth**, *which is a poem featured in Calgary's Poet Laureate legacy project,* **YYC POP: Portraits of People**. *Danielle Paul's debut poetry collection—***Dividing Flowers From Weeds***—is available on bksinbed.com. You can find her on Instagram @danielle.la.vue to see more work and for updates on future projects.*

THE WISE MEN OF THE EAST:

HOW THREE ZOROASTRIAN PRIESTS FOUND
THE PROMISED MESSIAH IN THE DAYS OF KING HEROD

JAY TYSON

I t was a bold move from any perspective... but not an irrational one.

To set out on a journey by camel to a city over a thousand miles away on the strength of a religious prophecy that was a thousand years old— well, some called it foolhardy. Some were amazed. Others were worried about what these Zoroastrian priests—or Magi as they were called in the days when the Bible was written—might find.

They had their own expectations, to be sure. Their Prophet, Zoroaster, Who had lived a thousand years earlier, had assured His followers that the Wise Lord (or, in the language of the time, *"Ahura Mazda"*) would send a new Messenger or *Saoshyant*—once in about a thousand years, for the next three thousand years at least. So, these Magi lived at a time of high millennial expectations.

It was Melichior[1] who first proposed setting forth in a search. His younger friends, Caspar and Balthazar, were entranced by the idea. But Caspar wondered, "How do we know that this is exactly the right year?" (For their

---

1   The author is aware that the names of the Wise Men, or even their number, as well as the name of the town from which they came and several other details, are not mentioned in the Bible but rather have been drawn from various traditions and accounts. They are adopted here to simplify the telling of this short story.

scriptures—at least those that had survived Alexander's onslaught—had not been very specific on this point.)

Balthazar added, "Where should we search?" The remnants of their scripture suggested various possibilities.

"Both good points," conceded Melichior, "and I would not set out on such a search unless I saw a sign amid the stars as Zoroaster had predicted. We should simply pray for guidance from the Wise Lord."

They knew that they would receive no assistance from the Parthian leaders who now ruled their country, whose zeal for the religion of Zoroaster was lukewarm at best. No, they would have to do this search on their own.

It was about a year later that the hoped-for sign appeared. A brilliant comet had appeared low in the western sky. Day after day, it was seen in the evening sky, pointing westward. "Yes, that is our sign," announced Melichior to his friends, "and that is our direction!"

They knew, of course, the history of their people and their faith. They knew that the spiritual teachings of Zoroaster had spread gradually among the people of Persia, strengthening their character. Upon noble and trustworthy people—good in thought, good in speech and good in action, as Zoroaster had taught—great civilizations could be built. The Achaemenid dynasty had arisen on this foundation, and Cyrus the Great had extended this great Persian Empire nearly six centuries before the days of Jesus. As it expanded outward, it had taken over Babylon and all of the lands over which the Babylonians had ruled, including the land of Israel. It had also taken over all of the Babylonian captives, including the Israelites. In the Israelites, Cyrus and his dynasty had found a spiritual kinship, for these people, like the Zoroastrians (but unlike almost everyone else in the ancient world), believed that there was only one supreme God. Cyrus's wisdom was praised in the Hebrew Bible. He and his dynasty released the Jewish people from the captivity which the Babylonians had imposed, encouraged them to return to their land, and to rebuild Jerusalem, which was still under the territorial control of Persia at that time. So, when the comet pointed to the west, the Magi naturally understood this to mean that they should travel to the capital of that nation and inquire about the spiritual King who was to be born there.

As they commenced the 40-day journey from Saveh in Persia, passing westward through the Zagros Mountains, they discussed their expectations and concerns.

"He will be born of a virgin," mentioned Melichior, "for this is one of the signs mentioned in our Holy Book, the Avesta."

"He will have innate knowledge," said Balthazar, "just as Zoroaster had."

"He will begin His mission with a conference with God at the age of 30," said Caspar, recalling a quotation to that effect from the Avesta.

They discussed other things they anticipated, such as His being a king, His speaking with the voice of God, and His suffering.

"But," cautioned Melichior, "if my understanding is correct, the sign of the star appears at the time of His birth. And thus, we may not be able to witness some of the signs, which will appear only later in His life, or after His death."

With thoughts such as these, they crossed across the plains of the great Tigris and Euphrates Rivers and then traversed the foreboding deserts of Arabia—their sense of anticipation growing with every passing day. At each sunset, they saw the comet, westward-pointing and a little higher in the sky, providing a feeling that they were drawing nearer to their goal.

From Damascus, they descended to the Sea of Galilee and, following the Jordan River southward, they reached Jerusalem as the comet, when viewed at sunset, was nearing its zenith. Here was the ancient capital of the Jewish realm—the seat of the Jewish kings. What better place to find the King of the Jews?

But, in meeting with King Herod and explaining the reason for their quest, they were chagrined to hear that there were no reports of the appearance of the promised Messenger nor a budding king. The king was still helpful: He summoned his chief priests and scribes, and they ascertained that the best place to search was in nearby Bethlehem, less than a day's journey further south. So the king sent them on their way and requested that they report back whatever they found. They soon set out, disappointed that they had found nothing in Jerusalem but hopeful that they might find the Object of their quest in Bethlehem, as the Jewish scripture had foretold.

That evening at sundown, the comet seemed to be hovering directly overhead. Asking one of the townspeople if they had heard of anything unusual that recently happened, they quickly heard the miraculous story of the angels who had appeared to some shepherds less than two weeks earlier. The news was on everyone's lips. And so that evening—the twelfth night since the Lord had been born—they were ushered into the place where the Christ Child, Mary, and Joseph were staying. There, beholding a Child whose countenance was beaming with light, they immediately fell down and worshipped in adoration of the Child. His appearance reminded them so perfectly of the ancient stories they had heard about the glowing light which emanated from Zoroaster at the time of His birth.

After this great homage, they listened with rapt attention to all that Mary had to say about the wondrous events that had led up to this point. The angel's announcement to Mary and the fact that she had been "touched by no man" confirmed beyond any doubt that this was the event promised by Zoroaster. Their hearts were soaring, firstly because of the wonderous news of the appearance of the new *sayoshyant* but doubly because of how clearly this proved the astounding accuracy of Zoroaster's prophetic ability.

When Mary asked them to tell the story of what had brought them to this place, Melichior told of the promises in their own Holy Book and how the promised star in the west had guided them. At the end, all of them paused with a sense of awe, thinking of the amazing power and the knowledge of the Almighty, Who was able to bring them all together in spite of the vast distances that separated them. Mary pondered in her heart how the God of the Jewish people must also be the God of these priests and their people, and how He was, indeed, the God of the entire earth.

The visitors brought forth their gifts and the explanations connected to each of them.

"He will be a king," said Caspar, "and thus I have brought a gift of gold, suitable for a king."

"As with our Prophet," said Balthazar, "He will not fear suffering nor even His own death and will accept these at the hands of His persecutors. As a symbol of this, I have brought myrrh—the ointment for the deceased."

"He will speak with the voice of God, revealing truths from the spiritual realms," added Melichior, "even as Zoroaster did. And thus, I have brought a gift of frankincense as a symbol of inspiration from the spiritual realm."

And so they spoke well into the night.

But that night, Melichior's sleep was interrupted by the appearance of an angel, warning him of King Herod's devious plans. The following day, as they began their preparations for the return trip, they chose a new route which did not pass through Jerusalem.

As they followed the long road back home and discussed the amazing things they had discovered, they wondered how the people of Persia would react to the news they brought. And how would the other magi respond?

"They will surely be exuberant and joyful," said Balthazar. "The accuracy of the prophecy of Zoroaster is now clear for all to see! What greater joy could anyone find?"

Caspar was not so certain. "The Child we found, and the stories we have heard concerning His conception and birth are undeniably amazing to us," he said, "but will they appear so to our people? What of those who have expected to see a wealthy king in royal robes? What will they say when we report that the Child was born in a manger where the animals feed? When we explain that He will be raised in the home of a common carpenter rather than in a royal court, what will the people think? What of those who expected a mighty warrior, who would free us from the threat of invading armies? How will they understand when we speak of a Child whose home is not even within the Zoroastrian realms? Alas, our people have many expectations, which are either their own interpretations of things they have heard from Zoroaster's teachings or they are simply from their own imaginations. Will these people be able to open their spiritual eyes and understand the spiritual truths behind Zoroaster's teachings and prophecies?"

Melichior thought even further. "The teachings of Zoroaster brought about many changes in His day. Many of the old ways and ideas were overturned, and with them, many of the positions of power were changed as well. I suspect," he said ominously, "that some—or maybe most—of our fellow magi may treat this news we bring more as a threat than as a blessing. In the arising of this

Child, they may see the possible decline of their own positions of prestige and power. Thus, like the leaders of the old Mazdayasnian religion in the time of Zoroaster Himself, we may find that the leaders of the old ways in our times are reluctant to yield to anything new."

Indeed, Melichior's words proved to be prescient. For it is now evident that, although they carried this great good news back to the people of Persia, it generated few if any followers—certainly not enough to start a substantial Christian community which later missionaries would find. It would be at least a century before Christian missionaries would be able to establish any significant communities there. After another century, the Zoroastrian religion would become closely associated with the new Sasanian Empire. Ninety years later, the Christian religion would become closely associated with the Roman Empire. Thus the animosity between these two humanmade empires would begin to percolate into the two monotheistic religions that had provided their spiritual foundations.

And yet, the story of the successful search of the Wise Men persists. It remains a testimony to the fact that the knowledge of the truth of Jesus extended beyond the cultural or historic limitations of the world of Judaism and to the fact that the ability to make startlingly accurate prophecies was not confined to the prophets of the Bible alone.

∞

Jay Tyson grew up outside of Detroit, Michigan, and graduated from Princeton University with a degree in Civil Engineering in 1976. Shortly thereafter he married Eileen Cregge. They spent four years in Liberia, West Africa, where Jay worked on road construction projects. They settled in Haifa, Israel, for seven years, where he assisted with historic restoration at the Baha'i World Center. They returned to New Jersey in 1989, where they raised two daughters, and Jay continued his career in engineering and began exploring religion. In addition to his research and writing, Jay is an active proponent of the Baha'i Faith as he recognizes the commonalities across religious traditions.

SUMMER KNIGHT
KELSEY HUMPHREY

S he let her dark hair come undone, much to her dismay. She quite liked it up, but you must do what you must. She strode over to the dance floor, her long black hair swaying as she walked. She was on a mission. Find the girl. Find the girl. Find the girl. And there she was, blonde hair shining under the lights. That was easy enough. The blonde turned around and smiled at the other girl.

"Hey, angel," she slurred. She was obviously intoxicated.

"Nessa," the raven-haired girl corrected.

"Nessa," the blonde purred. "What a name."

"Listen," Nessa began, shaking off her feelings; she had come here for a reason. "People are looking for you."

"People always are," the blonde said, still running her eyes up and down Nessa. "My name's Summer."

"We've met, remember? That night on the roof..." Nessa sighed. "Look, Summer, I'm serious. These people...I'm sure you've heard how dangerous they are."

"Dangerous smangerous," said Summer. "Let's dance."

Nessa barely had time to respond before Summer grabbed her hand and pulled her in close. The problem was that neither of the girls was a very good dancer. Many toes were stepped on. Nessa and Summer laughed for what seemed like forever, though it was still not enough time. Nessa knew their time would run out sooner rather than later. This bliss couldn't last long. She pulled

Summer closer to her, murmured in her ear, and told her the whole story about what was going on.

Summer pulled away and went to sit down.

Nessa followed her. "I know it's a lot to process."

"A lot to process?" Summer exclaimed, her voice hoarse. "You're telling me I could die at any moment!"

"Yes, but that's why I'm here, to protect you…" Nessa began "I mean, you're perfectly capable, but even I couldn't fend off these Big Bads by myself without a team."

Summer met Nessa's eyes, teardrops streaming down her face. "So, you're saying we're a team?"

"Of course, we are."

Summer put her hand over Nessa's and beamed.

* * *

Summer and I have been a team for about two weeks now. Maybe I should explain who we're on the run from exactly.

You see, Summer is special, and I'm not just saying that because I…because I care about her. Summer Knight comes from a very important family. She's the only child from this family now, and a lot of people would love to see her head on a silver platter—people like Ian James and his evil crew, for example.

But why do I care? Let's just say my family owes the Knight family. It's a long story we really don't have time for.

Why are the Knights so important? Summer and I live in a small town in Kentucky, called Dose, not so far from Louisville. Summer's mother is in politics; she's currently the mayor of Dose and is trying to do a lot of good with her position. But not everyone sees it that way. Kentucky is a pretty red state after all, so when a Democrat is elected, you can imagine how that could upset some.

Anyways, to me it's okay to have differing opinions, but Ian James and his…cult…are a different story. They are relentless with their views, giving Republicans a pretty bad name. The worst thing they did was assassinate Summer's dad. It was a year ago, around the time May Knight was elected. They never served time for their crime, but everyone knows it was them.

So, both Knight women have targets between their eyes. I feel like it's my job to protect them, because who else will? The police? Fat chance.

"Ness!"

I'm snapped out of my thoughts by the sound of Summer's voice calling my name, music to my ears...

"What's up?" I say.

"Nessie, didn't you hear that?" Summer whispers. I look over at her, she's standing, frozen, staring at the front door with her wide brown eyes.

I rise to my feet immediately. "Hear what?"

"I—I don't know" she stammers, and I see she's crying silent tears.

I put a comforting arm around her. "I'll go check it out, yeah?"

She throws both arms around my neck fiercely. "Be careful."

After I untangle myself, I grab the sharpest kitchen knife I can find and make my way toward the front door. I open it and find—absolutely nothing. There's no one there. I turn back to face Summer. "I don't see any— "

Summer catches me before I can hit the floor. There's an excruciating pain in my lower back, as if I've been stabbed and oh—oh I realize I have been stabbed.

"Nessa, no!" I can faintly hear Summer as she sobs. I can feel myself gently being set down.

"Knife..." I whisper.

Summer's already holding my discarded knife and charging outside. She's met by none other than Ian James himself.

"Oh no!" he says, his voice dripping with sarcasm. "Oops! Did I do that?"

Summer screams, a scream of fury, and charges at him, a tactic he swiftly avoids. His disgusting laughter fills the air.

"You're going to have to do a little better than tha-" His words are cut off, as is his left pinky finger.

While he screams over the loss of his finger, Summer comes behind him and stabs him, right where he stabbed me. "For Nessa," she hisses and yanks the knife away as Ian crumples to the floor.

I couldn't see all this go down, but I can just imagine how badass Summer must've looked. I can hear Ian James choking on his own blood as Summer rushes over to me.

"Nessa, baby, oh my god, there's so much blood!" she's crying again, this time audibly.

"Did—did you really not remember our night on the roof?" I blurt out.

Summer makes a noise that's half-sob, half-laugh. "My Nessa..." she cries. "How could I ever forget?"

I see she's on the phone with 911 before I close my eyes, my head spinning, my thoughts filled with Summer. Summer laughing, Summer smiling, Summer saying I'm hers. I am.

"Summer...." I whisper.

"Ness," she says, "save your energy. The ambulance is on the way."

"There's something I needed—I need to say." My eyes fly open to meet Summer's. "Before...if I—"

"No!" Summer says, her grip on my hand growing tighter. "Not an option. We're a team remember?"

"*Te amo*, Summer. My Summer, even in Winter."

She looks at me for a while, my eyes flutter shut again. Maybe I shouldn't have... And then she's kissing me. My hands, my forehead, then my lips, ever so gently.

"*Te amo*, Nessie," she whispers against my lips, then the sound of sirens fills our ears.

∾

*Kelsey Humphrey is an aspiring writer from Kentucky. Her two self-published poetry collections, **Bile** and **Vile**, are available on Amazon. She is currently working on her third collection, **Mile**. You can find her @kelshumphrey on Instagram and Twitter!*

CHARCOAL MOONS

L.S. BLACK

I t's not a nightmare.

It doesn't feel like a nightmare. Nightmares have this unreality that is weaved into them; impossible things that don't concern you at the time but upon waking, you know that they were utterly unbelievable. Even the most bizarre storylines become plausible in your sleeping mind. Panic and confusion rise from the total acceptance that what you are sensing is actually happening. It's not. You wake in your darkened room with a thudding pulse, and you realise that it was just a dream... and how silly it was too. Throughout the day, your mind cleanses all the uncomfortable memories of its absurd storyline until you can hardly recall what it was that had made you wake with heavy panting breath in the first place.

Perhaps this is a haunting? There is no ominous entity grown from superstition or a misunderstood history, though; no figure trapped in a fleeting moment in time and unable to accept its current state of being.

Is it a malevolent force conjured up by an unquenchable thirst for revenge, strung tight to some mediocre *objet d'art* I had picked up at a garage sale? He doesn't seem like a spectral presence that fuels the most captivating stories on my bookshelves.

No. He has scent, weight, sound, and taste.

This is whole.

This is conscious.

This feels real.

* * *

"Hypnopompic hallucinations, Miss Cole. Very real at the time, but it's nothing more than parts of your brain finding it hard to get up in the morning." Pencil-thin lips, painted in a conservative maroon, stretched into a basic smile that revealed the blush wrinkles where the lipstick hadn't made it into the cracks. I blinked a few times to re-centre my eyes on the doctor's.

"Hypno...?"

"...Pompic. Hallucinations upon waking up. It's hypnagogic if they come as you fall asleep." She turned away from me. "Your brain doesn't wake up enough to stop the dream or let you move, but the rest of you is functioning as normal."

"But I sense him. I can feel him. Smell him."

"In the dream, you do, of course. I'll start by dropping the strength of your sedatives to see if that allows you to wake up easier. I also suggest you continue with your breathing exercises for stress relief." She handed me the prescription. The only stress in my life was trying to explain to various doctors that what I saw every night was not stress or tablet side-effects.

Every new doctor had a new, mild theory. First was lack of sleep, and recently it was too much sleep. They said it was food allergies, technology overuse, blue light, lack of water, depression, and anxiety. All of the doctors spoke with good intentions and a look in their eye that said they were confused by how sane I came across, and therein lay the problem.

I think I'm crazy, and no one believes me.

* * *

I arrived home and shed my coat over the back of the sofa with an exaggerated sigh. Toby was already home from work and making a mess of the kitchen as he busied himself with making a snack.

"Hey, how'd it go?" he asked as he butchered a slice of bread with a lump of butter and a steak knife. I rolled my eyes and took over, wielding a butter knife like a surgeon as I struggled to save the mangled bit of crust.

"Hypnopompic hallucinations, apparently."

"Hallucinations? So, you are mental then?"

I shot him a disapproving look; he just laughed.

"It's a waking dream. This doctor thinks it's because of the tablets."

"But they gave you the tablets to help with the dream in the first place."

"I know. I know. I'm just tired of arguing with doctors and specialists. I think…" I paused, spreading the butter as I mulled over my next words. "…I think I'm just going to have to learn to live with this."

"Okay. I mean, loads of people dream, so it's not going to kill you. It's just unpleasant, like farting during sex."

"For crying out loud, Toby." I pushed the plate of buttered bread towards him and made my exit from the kitchen. "And it's not a dream."

"Well, what do I call it?" He shouted after me, his voice already muffled by half-chewed food. I didn't answer.

* * *

I don't dream anymore. I don't lose my teeth while trying in vain to jab out a phone number with suddenly inflating fingers, nor do I get to fly over scrawling skyscrapers. I just get *him*. Never quite the same, yet always just as real.

I lay in bed. Toby was already snoring faintly from somewhere in the darkness beside me, and I thought about the first time it happened.

I had spent the afternoon shopping with some friends and arrived home weary but looking forward to a glass of wine and a romantic chick flick. I lived alone then. Toby hadn't yet breezed into my life, and I was happy with my independent evenings of solitude. Rain lashed at the skylight window, and along with the red wine, it eased me into a sound and very plain slumber.

When I stirred from sleep, I was aware that it was still dark but early enough to promise a few more hours of sleep. I was on my back, and the faintest outline of light was creeping through the door frame from the hallway—a pale square of night sky from the skylight above. It didn't take long for the dim light to bring the usual outlines of my bedroom into view from the inky black. Nothing felt out of place except that it was silent.

Very silent.

I couldn't hear the gentle movement of the covers as I breathed. I couldn't hear the air flowing through my nostrils. I couldn't even hear the constant march of my heartbeat as the blood flowed past my eardrums. The silence draped over me in this cold blanket of confusion; my brain struggled to accept it.

That's when the shadow to the left of the door caught my eye. A startled leap of fear rushed into my chest and stung. It looked as if something, no, someone, was sitting, hunched over on my ottoman. The feeble light from the cracks around the door painted a deep maroon outline of what seemed to be legs emerging from heavy boots, knees, torso, square shoulders, and a head... a head bent low to keep the features of the face in utter darkness. I blinked in the hope that a crumpled coat might develop from the shape instead, a simple trick of the light and sleepy eyes.

The figure's silhouette remained.

Even more alarming was that it had a sense of movement to it. It wasn't static and frozen but seemed to move in such a minute way as if it were breathing, as if it were alive. This is where the horror stories would explain how I couldn't move no matter how much I tried, but the truth is I never once attempted to move. My heart pounded away unheard in my chest, and I didn't think to react in any other way than being utterly solid and silent.

I was aware that I was breathing rapidly and that I missed three breaths when the figure rose from its seat.

Then I saw them. Two dark circles looking straight at me, the dim glint of light reflected from glossy charcoal moons.

I closed my eyes, trying to wake from what I desperately wanted to be a dream, but I opened them again, without reason, to watch him edge closer.

My eyes searched for something to assure myself it was a nightmare, though everything except him seemed just how it should be. I could feel the soft brushed cotton of the sheet beneath my hands, the wooden button on my pillowcase that dug into my shoulder, and the cold parts of the duvet that touched my skin as the figure began to climb up onto my bed.

The weak light now illuminated his lack of face. The charcoal moons were the dark glass circles of an old gas mask. The thick black rubber clinging tight to his unseen features, the long ribbed tube trailed from where his mouth should have been and vanished to somewhere within his coat.

The first sensation of his touch took my breath away as the cracked leather of his glove snaked under the side of the covers and scratched the skin on my thigh. It only moved when he continued to slide his heavy body on top of mine. The sheets trapped me like bindings beneath his weight. My feet felt the cold night air as the covers rode up and the wet mud that rubbed off of his boots as they knocked painfully against my ankles.

Tears stung at the back of my throat and deep in my nose. He leaned in, and I tried to shrink back from the musty, damp smell of his coat that sprinkled remnants of the rain onto my chest. His gloved hands caught my hair as he placed them either side of my head.

I could smell the rust from the silver rings around those empty glass voids and the putrid rubber of old car tires from the mask. The ribs of the pipe rubbed against my quivering lips until I could taste the plastic.

Then there was a sound as if it exploded from the silence. My heart, the covers, my breath and his, rasping and rattling through the pipe.

Inhale. Exhale. Inhale. Exhale.

He started to retreat, and I felt hot liquid surround my buttocks as I wet myself. He backed into the corner and lowered himself back onto the ottoman.

Inhale. Exhale.

I was too frightened to look away. I just watched him, and he watched me for what felt like hours. The light morning sky crept in, and the brighter the room became, the more invisible he became.

Eventually, I rolled over, held myself, and sobbed.

It was even longer before I had enough courage to move from the bed. At first, it was to sit up and grab my phone to call the police, and I swiped aside the barrage of missed calls and notifications from being late to work. The wet sheets beneath me made the tears come tainted with shame.

I stopped mid-dial.

Things about my room made me doubt what had just happened. The door was neatly closed with a discarded pair of knickers against them, exactly where I had lazily kicked them off before bed. The lilac carpet was free of mud, and a neat stack of clothes was piled on the ottoman where the figure had been sitting.

I crept out of the bedroom with a high heel held to my chest as a deadly weapon of protection and investigated the rest of my apartment. Not a single thing was out of place. No sign of entry; no indication he was ever there. Confused and still shaking, I called my mother and sobbed the story of my night to her.

The police said it was probably a vivid dream. Sleepover friends, cameras, and eventually Toby confirmed it was all "just a dream."

* * *

I was disturbed from my memories when Toby's gentle snoring stopped. The wind outside stopped. The sound of my heartbeat stopped.

He's early tonight.

Inhale. Exhale.

I searched the darkness of the room and found the two identical glints in the dark. Those charcoal moons, looming directly above me.

Inhale.

He's closer tonight.

Exhale.

The worldly sounds sweep in across the room like a wave, the wind returns to buffer against the windows, and a whisper comes from beside me that makes my skin prickle. Those black glass circles move slowly to watch a new target. It was Toby's voice from beside me in the dark, small and shaking, choked with swallowed tears and disbelief.

"I see him too."

Aspiring author of horror and speculative fiction, L.S. Black is currently working towards a degree in Creative Writing and English Literature.

CPSIA information can be obtained
at www.ICGtesting.com
Printed in the USA
BVHW040216181121
621918BV00019B/385